THE PASSIONATE DELEGATE

THE PASSIONATE DELEGATE

UNSTOPPABLE LIV BEAUFONT™ BOOK 9

SARAH NOFFKE

MICHAEL ANDERLE

This book is a work of fiction.

All of the characters, organizations, and events portrayed in this novel
are either products of the author's imagination or are used fictitiously.
Sometimes both.

LMBPN Publishing
PMB 196, 2540 South Maryland Pkwy
Las Vegas, NV 89109

First US Edition, July 2019
Version 1.01, August 2019
Print ISBN: 978-1-64202-389-3

THE PASSIONATE DELEGATE TEAM

Thanks to the JIT Readers

Nicole Emens
Crystal Wren
Daniel Weigert
Larry Omans
Jeff Goode
Kelly O'Donnell
Jeff Eaton
Deb Mader
Peter Manis
Misty Roa
Micky Cocker
Angel LaVey

If I've missed anyone, please let me know!

Editor
The Skyhunter Editing Team

For Trudy.
The first day we met, you called me a tiger.
Still my favorite college class ever. And the one that flamed my
fire for writing.
— Sarah

To Family, Friends and
Those Who Love
to Read.
May We All Enjoy Grace
to Live the Life We Are
Called.
— Michael

The stench inside the old gas station was almost worse than the smell of rotting catfish and mildew out front. The sign for Jeb's Trading Post had fallen into disrepair ages ago, by the looks of it. Thankfully Kayla Sinclair had other ways of locating the rusty filling station. The person she'd spoken to had said there would be a red swivel chair out front with profanities written on the material. The people in the South used strange landmarks, she'd found in her travels.

Kayla kicked the chair over with her combat boot before entering the gas station, irritated by the long day of travel and humid weather in the backwoods outside New Orleans.

"The bathrooms are out back, darling," the pot-bellied man said from behind the counter, not looking up from his crossword puzzle.

"I know that already," Kayla answered, having checked out the property entirely before entering. The disgusting outhouse in the back shouldn't really be considered a proper place to relieve oneself, just like the one-legged rooster that was hopping around outside shouldn't really be considered a prized fighting cock.

The man behind the counter glanced up, obviously not used to young women frequenting his establishment. She guessed he only got smelly old fisherman and lost tourists. His aged eyes widened at the sight of her. It probably wasn't her modern hairstyle that gave him pause. Kayla wore her hair short and spikey on one side of her head and long on the other. The black mini skirt and tank top might have been what got his attention, but she doubted it.

"You're…you one of those really white people," the hick exclaimed.

Kayla released a deep breath and raised her hands, about to lay them on the sticky counter separating them. Then she thought better of it and kept her hands by her sides.

"Albino," she supplied.

He chuckled and slid his pencil behind his ear. "Well, I'll be. I've never seen one of you before. Heard about you folks, though. Are you looking for the sunscreen?" He glanced around, his brow furrowed. "I ain't restocked that in some time. You might try the Walmart back twenty miles from here."

Kayla shook her head, trying to keep her temper quelled. Talon Sinclair had told her what to do and ordered her not to draw much attention to herself. That was never easy. Everyone always remembered her, either because of how she looked or what she made them see.

"Are you Jeb Navarro?" she asked the man.

He smiled, sticking his hands into the pockets of his

overalls. "That would be me, darling. What can I do you for?"

"I'm looking for Zeno Dutillet," she said, enjoying the way the Cajun French name rolled off her tongue.

The man started as if he'd suddenly been pushed. "How'd you hear about him? Ain't no one asked about him in some time."

"I heard he was here," she said plainly.

The door she'd come through swung open, the bell attached to it chiming like it was suddenly angry. Kayla kept her eyes on the old man even as the hot wind from outside rushed through the small store.

"He's in the back," the clerk said, indicating with his head. "But no one's come around for him in…well, ever."

"I need to wake him," Kayla said, stepping to the side and leaning around to look in the back. There wasn't much there. A small room for restocking. Maybe a closet or two.

Jeb shook his head furiously. "Oh, no. You can't do that. Zeno Dutillet has been asleep for…well, all my life. My daddy's life too. My kinsfolk have been charged with keeping him that way."

Yes, the Navarro family. They'd been doing their job well for quite some time, but that was all about to change.

"Your job is done," Kayla said, making for the back.

Jeb stepped in front of her, halting her progress. "I'm sorry, ma'am, but I can't allow you to do that. I don't know what happens when Zeno Dutillet is stirred, but I ain't going to risk it."

She batted her white eyelashes at him. "Oh, it's nothing. Just blissful sleep. You'll love it."

He shook his head more forcefully this time. "Nah. I've

been told that if anyone ever came trying to wake Zeno Dutillet, I had to do everything in my power to stop them."

The portly man was surprisingly fast for his size, reaching for something on the shelf on the side of the wall. In a flash, he was aiming a shotgun straight at Kayla's face.

She sighed, realizing she might have to actually get her hands dirty for this one.

"I don't want any trouble," the man said. "Just walk back out the way you came in, and we can forget about this."

Kayla held her hands up as if in surrender, but really it was only so she was ready to attack. "The thing is that I can't forget about Zeno Dutillet or why I've come to wake him. I have my orders."

"And I have mine," the redneck said, narrowing his eyes at her.

"Then we will do this the hard way," she said and flicked her hand ever so slightly. The man flew backward, knocking into a shelf full of bait. A loud crack was followed by him sliding to the floor and the shelves overhead breaking. Buckets of worms and other rancid-smelling bait spilled onto the man's head before he could rise, and his gun fell to the floor.

Kayla was about to march into the back when the sounds of running footsteps made her pause.

"Stop right there!" someone yelled from behind her.

She flexed her fingers by her sides, ever so slightly glancing over her shoulder. Two men had entered the shop.

"Leave, or you die," she threatened flatly.

The old man was trying to stand but kept slipping on the muck underfoot. Annoyed by the whole thing, Kayla lifted her hand, and the clerk rose with it. His legs kicked as he tried to find stable ground, but he rose ever farther. With a jerk of her hand, Kayla sent the man's head into the ceiling, which was rotted in places from storms and the constant moisture.

Jeb screamed, his limbs flailing. His head remained stuck above the ceiling, and his bottom half hung down.

Kayla heard a click behind her; she knew that sound. One of the men behind her had chambered a bullet, which meant he'd be the first to die.

She swung around, bringing her arm out wide with her. The canned goods, fishing lures, and hooks lining one wall flew off and straight at the man holding the gun. They assaulted him one after the other, many of the sharper objects stabbing him. When a can of dog food hit him in the side of the head, he stumbled back, shielding his face, which had multiple hooks in it. The objects kept rising off the ground again and racing back for his face or chest or wherever they could make contact.

The man beside him, the youngest of the three watched in horror, unable to do anything to save him. Finally, the battered man gave up, throwing his rifle on the floor of the shop and running for the exit, many of the objects racing after him.

Kayla lowered her chin, regarding the last remaining man with her nearly white eyes. "Stay, and you die. Leave, and you live."

With a frantic look in his eyes, he swung his head over his shoulder. Then he spun in that direction, making for the door.

She laughed, flicking her wrist to the right hard. The

running man froze, his neck jerking awkwardly to the side. A loud crack emanated from the man as his spine cracked in two. His head lolled to the side strangely before he collapsed on the floor.

Kayla shook her head. She was never going to allow any of these men to live. Before she awoke Zeno Dutillet, she'd finish off the other two. The one hanging from the ceiling would be easy to kill. The one who had fled, well, the objects she sent after him wouldn't stop assaulting him until he was dead. That was the beauty of the "Merciless Object" curse. It did all the work for Kayla and didn't quit until its target was no longer moving.

Killing everyone in the Navarro family was key. They were the only ones who could currently put Zeno Dutillet back to sleep, according to the lore. Yes, another family would be chosen, Kayla was sure, but it would be too late by then. Zeno Dutillet only needed to be awake for a short time to do the damage Talon Sinclair wanted.

Kayla held her hand underneath Jeb Navarro's still-flailing limbs. He was close to getting his fat head unstuck from the plaster.

With no remorse, she closed her fist, and Jeb screamed and reached for his chest. A moment later, he was completely still, the heart attack having been swift and deadly.

Kayla dropped her hand back to her side, sizing up the ransacked shop with a proud smile. She turned toward the back room, where Zeno Dutillet was sleeping.

It was time to wake the SandMan.

CHAPTER TWO

"I really don't get it," John said, scratching his head and regarding the microwave oven with confusion. "We've checked the fuses, the interlock safety switches, and discharge capacitor. Nothing seems to be wrong with this thing."

Yes, they'd spent the better part of the morning wracking their brains over a seemingly trivial thing—a repair for a thirty-dollar microwave. Yes, there were many other things that Liv should be doing. But right then, working on the microwave with John Carraway was keeping her sane. There were few activities Liv enjoyed more than repairing things with John.

"You know, we might want to consider that there's no fixing this one," she said, having looked the machine over a hundred times. She was still unable to determine what was wrong with it.

John shook his head. "Yeah, sometimes things just wear out, and there's no fixing them." He let out a long breath and sat down in the folding chair beside the workstation. "I sort of feel like this microwave lately."

Liv's gaze shot to the old man, who was breathing harder than he should. "Don't talk like that."

He chuckled. "Well, it's true. Haven't been feeling like myself lately. Maybe it's the extra pollen in the air or—"

"That you're visiting the taco truck too often," she cut in.

His face flushed red with guilt. "Well, I went on Monday, and the carnitas didn't give me indigestion."

"So you went back every day this week?" Liv asked, her tone flaring.

"Well, the chicken did give me heartburn on Tuesday so I thought I'd try the carne asada on Wednesday. When that wasn't a problem—"

"I'm not sure I need a full run-through on the week," Liv interrupted. "Keep a food journal and try to eat some vegetables."

John grimaced. "I thought you wanted me to live a long, happy life?"

"Yes, hence the reason for the insistence that you eat broccoli and brussels sprouts."

"Well, then I might live a long life, but it won't be happy," John stated just as the phone rang on the workstation.

Liv couldn't help but notice how John's eyes brightened as he read the caller ID.

"Alicia De Luca, eh?" Liv asked, arching a curious eyebrow at him. She was surprised to see the magic tech scientist from Venice was calling John on his phone.

"We stay in contact," he said, pressing the phone to his

chest as it continued to ring. "You know, exchange tips on electronic repair."

"Sure, sure," Liv said, a hint of mischief in her tone.

He waved her off. "Oh, just because you're all twitter-pated after that tall, handsome fellow doesn't mean the rest of us are."

"Then where are you going?" Liv asked as he disappeared into the back.

"Just don't want to disturb you while you work," he called as the door swung shut behind him.

"Yeah, right," Liv said with a laugh. She liked Alicia, and she loved John. If two people she cared about could find a friendship together, well, it was a win-win for her.

"You're avoiding your problems," Plato said, materializing beside her as soon as John was out of earshot.

She ducked, peering at the back of the microwave. "No, my problem is right here. I just can't figure it out."

Plato lifted his paw, eyeing it before taking a long lick like it was a lollypop. "Don't you think there are bigger issues out in the world that need your attention?"

"Like other microwaves that mysteriously don't work?" Liv asked.

"Like an entire population of mortals who are waking up and seeing magic for the first time."

She shook her head. "My job is recruiting the Mortal Seven. The council's job is helping mortals assimilate once they study the Forgotten Archives."

"Excuse me for being so bold, but I'm not sure how fixing Mr. Patrick's microwave gets you any closer to finding the Mortal Seven."

Liv scowled at the lynx before opening the door to the

microwave and peering inside. "Firstly, this is one of my jobs, and I can't just abandon it. And secondly, I don't even know where to look to find the Mortal Seven; well, asides from John. And even when I do find one of the families, I'm not sure what to do next. Do I just randomly point at the one who looks the nicest and say, 'Hey, you've been chosen as Councilor for the House of Fourteen. Congratulations! Drop everything you're doing. Magic needs your help.'"

"You might want to buy them a cup of coffee first," Plato suggested.

"I'll keep that sage advice in mind," Liv said with a grunt, peering once more into the open microwave.

"If you're looking for answers to this Mortal Seven business, I'm not sure they can be found inside of a smelly old microwave."

Liv jerked her head out and stood. "But are you sure?"

He sort of smirked. "Not entirely."

"So there!" she said victoriously. After a moment, she sighed in defeat. "And I know, you're right. Mortals are confused. Every day there are new reports of the strange things they are witnessing. We have to figure out how to explain to a few billion people why they are suddenly living in a very different world. The council has been meeting with groups from the different magical races to determine the best course of action, but these things take time. The important thing is that mortals are awake, they can see magic, and the forgotten history has been activated. It's a gradual process, having it weave itself back into the consciousness of mortals, magicians, and everyone else, but in time, it's supposed to be a part of our distant memories. Or at least, that's what Papa Creola states."

"Who are you talking to?" John asked from behind Liv.

She spun, looking for Plato, and shrugged when he wasn't anywhere around. "The cat. But he disappeared."

John gave her a sympathetic smile. "I know how much you want Plato to be your familiar."

"He is," Liv argued at once.

Again John flashed her a compassionate look. "It's just that sometimes a cat is just a cat. I'm sure, in your world, it's weird to have anything that is ordinary. I mean, Sophia has the dragon egg, and Alicia was once a chicken, and you see so many strange things every day."

"Exactly!" Liv stated. "So why is it so hard for you to believe that Plato is magical?"

John leaned over and patted his terrier, Pickles, on the head. "Because sometimes a cat is just a cat. Just as Pickles is just a dog. But I understand wanting him to be more."

"He is more," Liv argued. "He just doesn't show you because he likes to be a pain in the ass and it's against his religion to reveal himself to anyone but me."

"That's a weird religion," John said with a laugh.

"What did Alicia have to say?" Liv asked, her mood plummeting suddenly. Plato was right that she was hiding when she had other responsibilities. It was just that she was lost. After she defeated Adler and freed the mortals, everything was supposed to be perfect. It was supposed to go back to normal. But there was no normal. The Sinclairs had rewritten history and made the world a confusing place. Mortals were supposed to be able to see magic. They were the ones who governed it. However, a few centuries of having it locked away from them made it so the present reality was bizarre. How could mortals govern something they didn't understand and no one knew how to properly explain to them?

"Oh, not much, really," John said, averting his gaze from Liv's. "I told her about the microwave, and she gave me some suggestions to try."

"Maybe she'll stop by and have a look at it," Liv offered.

"Maybe," John said, a hint of excitement in his voice.

Liv was about to push the matter when her own phone rang. She eyed the caller ID with doubt. Her phone listed contacts whether she had them in her database or not. That was one of the perks of magical tech. However, she doubted it was correct in this instance.

"Hello?" Liv answered the phone. She was silent for a long moment while the person on the other side spoke. They didn't give her a moment to interject. Instead, they kept talking until they were done. "Ummm…yeah, I guess I can meet with you."

Without another word, the person on the other side hung up.

"What was that about?" John asked, curiosity brimming in his eyes.

"It was the President of the United States," she answered. "She wants to meet with me."

CHAPTER THREE

The portal to the White House stood in the middle of Liv's apartment, shimmering and giving off a soft melodic sound. She continued to stare at it impassively, not walking through as she was supposed to.

"I thought you'd be more excited about meeting the President," Stefan said, hiding the amused expression on his face.

"I am," she answered. "I just don't see why I have to dress like a court reporter to do it." Liv swept her arm at the black high heels that Sophia had magically put on her as a finishing touch to getting her ready. Then the little magician had taken her dragon egg to the back bedroom, stating that he was tired and ready for a nap.

"Puff the Magic Dragon lives in a thick shell, so I'm not sure why he can't nap…oh, I don't know, just about anywhere," Liv had said to her little sister's retreating back.

"That's not his name, and he says that your constant grumbling about having to brush your hair makes it difficult to relax." Sophia offered her one last look of sympathy before disappearing into her room with the large dragon egg.

Liv threw her hand through her freshly combed hair and sighed.

"I've never been to a mortal courtroom, but I'm not sure if you could get confused for a court reporter or a lawyer or anything close," Stefan said, eyeing her from the corner where he was propped against the wall, looking much more comfortable than her in his usual black attire and boots.

"Why do you think that is?" Liv glanced down at the black pencil skirt and blazer Sophia had magicked onto her, the material scratching her arms and legs.

Stefan pointed to Bellator, which she'd slung across her back. "It might be the giant-made sword. From what I've heard, mortals don't go to meet the President of the United States with swords. Their security frowns upon it."

Liv huffed. "Bellator calms me down and keeps me rational."

"I thought you said it also was hungry to feast on enemies' blood?" Stefan questioned.

"Which usually makes me feel like I'm not so crazy."

Stefan strode over and gingerly removed the sword from Liv's back. She allowed it, flashing him a look of dissatisfaction. She'd known it was unlikely that she'd be able to meet the President of the United States with a sword across her back, but it did make her feel better while the tight shoes were pinching her feet.

"If you want me to, I'll put on an equally uncomfortable outfit and accompany you," Stefan stated.

Liv considered that for a moment and shook her head.

"No. Strangely, your pain doesn't make me feel better. I thought that was how relationships work, but I guess I've got nothing figured out."

"Yes, I'm learning this all myself too," Stefan stated, carefully laying Bellator on the large dining room table. It had been a gift from Rory, who said she couldn't keep feeding Sophia on the carpet and calling it a picnic. "Apparently loving someone means wanting better for them than you want for yourself."

Liv narrowed her eyes. "Don't make me pick that sword up and use you as a sparring dummy."

The spark that radiated in Stefan's eyes when he smiled was full of just the right amount of playfulness. "Oh, did that L-word catch you off-guard? I apologize, my lady. I promise not to speak of my affections for you again until you're begging for them. Only then will I use terms that are to your liking."

Liv shook her head. "You're ridiculous. And you know you can't go with me. You've got elf negotiations to deal with. After this mortal business, we need the elves on our side. They can't go all rogue."

Stefan nodded confidently. "Don't you worry your well-combed head of hair. I've pretty much got this elf thing in the bag. I just need to catch one more bad guy, and the elves will be begging for an alliance."

"Okay, sounds like a plan," Liv said, taking a reluctant step toward the still-glowing portal. "You go slaughter a bad guy so we can form a partnership with the elves. Meanwhile, I'm just going to meet with the President of the United States."

"And then what do you say to some pad Thai and Netflix?" Stefan asked with a hint of mischief in his eyes.

"Don't try to domesticate me, Ludwig," she said, nearing the portal.

"What? If I had said nachos, you would have been all over the idea."

She shook her head at him. "Don't pretend you know me so well."

"I wouldn't dream of it."

Liv waved to him as she stepped through the portal, thinking how nice it would be to return home after a long day to nachos…and maybe even Stefan's face.

She let the idea linger a bit too long and was disoriented when she found herself stepping into the Oval Office a few seconds later.

The sound of a teacup shattering was the first thing Liv heard. Her hand reflexively went for Bellator before she remembered that she'd left it on her dining room table.

The President of the United States was regarding her with wide eyes, her mouth agape. On her lap was a beautiful saucer, the cup having fallen on it and broken. The tea was currently puddling in President Fuller's lap.

"Oh, I'm sorry, did I startle you?" Liv said, sweeping her hand through the air. The pieces of the broken teacup rose and came back together, and it looked pristine once more. With another swipe of her hand, Liv lifted the tea from the President's lap and deposited it in the cup.

The cup floated in the air between the President and Liv, bouncing around just a bit.

"I-I-I didn't expect you to enter that way," President

Fuller said. She had short blonde hair and was wearing an uncomfortable-looking outfit like Liv's.

"Yes, I guess I should have used the main entrance," Liv stated. "I just didn't want to go through security and all." She plucked the cup from midair and handed it to the President. "Here, I promise it's safe to drink. The same tea you were drinking. Not even a bit of lint from your clothes. I was careful."

President Fuller graciously took the cup, looking like she'd just swallowed a cookie without chewing. "You're a real magician then, aren't you?"

Liv nodded, looking around the Oval Office. "Yes. You've seen some really strange things lately, haven't you?"

The President set the teacup and saucer on the side table. "Actually, we're doing our best to change the stories that…our people are seeing. What is that you call us again?"

"Mortals," Liv supplied.

"Right," the President said. "Yes, I received the letter from the House of Fourteen. That's your ruling body, is that right?"

"Yes, in so many ways," Liv stated.

"They mentioned that you'd be working to recruit mortals who would preside over magical matters on this council of yours."

"That's right," Liv answered. "Although I haven't made much progress."

"Well, I'd like to make nominations for those who could represent mortals."

Liv shook her head. "I'm sorry, that's not how it works. The Mortal Seven have already been chosen."

"Oh? Then why haven't you made progress?"

"Because I don't know how to identify them yet," Liv stated.

President Fuller nodded like this made perfect sense. "This has been a very strange week. Finding out that magic is real and has always been around us is a lot to process. I'm having trouble dealing with this new history."

"It's the old history, actually," Liv corrected, pacing. She needed to expel her nervous energy, although her feet were already throbbing. "But I can only imagine what you and other mortals are going through. No one said this transition would be easy, but the hardest part is done. Mortals are awake after centuries of being blind to magic. They can help to keep the balance, which has been out of whack for too long. And I'm happy to help however I can. Now my question to you, President Fuller, is why did you call me here?"

When the President didn't reply, Liv turned to face her directly, wondering if she said something wrong that put her on edge. She blinked with confusion at the sight before her. It didn't appear that she'd said anything wrong, but rather had bored the President.

Lying across the sofa as if she'd laid down for an afternoon nap was the President of the United States. Her mouth opened, and she let out a very loud snore.

CHAPTER FOUR

After Liv stepped into the House of Fourteen, she took a step back out again. She had, in fact, gone through the right door. This was the entrance to the fake tarot card shop. And she wasn't drunk. Not yet, anyway. After boring the President of the United States to sleep, she was considering tying on a few after work, although there was never really any "after work" time. Still, she liked to play with the idea.

Liv stepped through the entrance again. It was absolutely stunning. The entryway to the House had been impressive before, especially after she became a Warrior and the long hallway was illuminated with the language of the Founders. Now it was simply breathtaking. The high, arched ceiling was decorated with intricate carvings that would have taken a craftsman a century to create by hand. The decorations ran the length of the hallway.

Carefully Liv took another step, noticing the plush red carpet under her feet. Pure gold sconces with flames lit the area. And marble statues lined the walls, which were still imbued with the language of the Founders. Fourteen statues.

The statues on the right were of the founding magicians, Liv realized at once. Something caught in her throat when she read the placard beside it:

Bernard Beaufont, Founder of the House of Fourteen.

That would have been Liv's great-great-great-grandfather. He was the one who had formed the House of Fourteen originally. She couldn't believe it. The history had been lost for so long that Liv hadn't known this. She knew the Beaufonts were one of three remaining founding families, but not that they were *the* founders.

Taking another step, she didn't need to read the placard beside the next statue to know it was of a member of the Takahashis. The magician was dressed as Akio and Haro often did, in traditional Japanese attire.

She stepped back in disgust at the next statue. It was of Talon Sinclair, and he had an uncanny resemblance to Adler. She hadn't regretted killing that man in the slightest, but seeing a face so similar to his did bring flashes of Adler's death to her mind's eye.

Turning to the other statues lining the opposite wall, Liv read the names of the Mortal Seven. They were the same ones she'd found in the ancient chamber.

Carloway
Reynolds
Luce
Alvarez
Gaumond
Wong
Fiori

Once she reached the end of the hallway, Liv found herself turning back and striding toward the entrance again. The House had changed because the truth had been revealed. She suddenly had a great fondness for the House of Fourteen, which was more alive than any place she'd ever known. It breathed. It grew. It slept. And when she least expected it, the House came alive. It was a person she'd known all her life, and one she hoped never to lose. Not now that she'd found such a deep appreciation for it.

"Isn't it ironic that you begrudgingly took on the role of Warrior for the House and now you relish the fact?" Plato asked, having materialized by her side.

She frowned. "It's rude to get into my head."

He strode beside her as she studied the statues again. "I'm not in your head. I am a figment of your imagination. And it was just a lucky guess."

"Really?"

"Yes, I don't actually exist, which is why no one else can see or hear me," Plato answered.

"That's not true. You've spoken to Clark before," Liv spat.

"Oh, really? You're going to legitimize my existence by using Clark? The guy you call a looney tune?" Plato asked.

"Right, good point. I knew I was insane." Liv halted after she'd once again come to the far end of the hallway. "I'm relieved you're not in my head because that would make you an even stranger imaginary friend."

"Yes, it would," Plato said. "And you didn't bore the President to sleep. I think there's something else at play there."

Liv's mouth popped open. "You *are* trespassing in my mind!"

She'd heard Plato speak to her from inside her head, like he was a part of her thoughts. She was only half-pretending to be offended. If anyone was going to read her mind, she was glad it was Plato.

"Maybe just a little bit," he admitted.

Liv studied the symbols, wondering if the message had changed, too. She pulled the Warrior ring from her pocket. Lately, she had it on her all the time, feeling that it kept her mother close to her somehow.

Running the ring over the symbols, she found that the message from before had stayed the same. Over and over, it said: "Stop the One, and you'll free us all."

"I don't get it," she said. "I killed Adler. Rory and Bermuda killed Decar. The evil Sinclairs are gone."

A perplexed expression crossed Plato's face. "Maybe they are referring to the Mortal Seven being freed. The message might remain the same until they've been located and appointed to the council."

"Maybe," Liv said, uncertainty in her voice.

Although she wanted to stay in the hallway and study the statues more, she forced herself to continue to the Chamber of the Tree. She was just about to step through the Door of Reflection when she noticed there were spots of color in the Black Void. Before it had only been swirling darkness with different shades of black. Now if she focused, Liv could see blues and greens and sparks of light.

"That's definitely new too," she said as she neared the Black Void, that feeling of impending doom growing stronger as she did.

A shock of electricity shot down Liv's spine suddenly, making her jump back. Protectively, Plato bolted in front of her, a cautious expression on his face.

"So that wasn't just my imagination?" Liv asked, panting like she'd just run several miles.

Plato shook his head. "No, I saw the shock. It looked like something was trying to come out of there."

"Oh, this is just perfect," Liv said dryly. "The cat who won't talk to anyone else is my only witness that there's something evil living in the Black Void, which no one else can see either."

"That doesn't at all sound like a perfect scenario," Plato said playfully.

"Ha-ha," Liv stated.

"For now, just stay away from it. The House is changing, and maybe this is how it's dispelling residual evil."

"I don't like it when you don't know about things since you seem to know about everything," Liv commented.

Plato agreed with a nod. "I don't like it either. It makes me feel like the rest of you."

Facing the Door of Reflection, Liv prepared herself for what she'd experience next. It was never easy to willingly walk into a nightmare. However, it was part of entering the Chamber of the Tree, and the experience had gotten easier. It was like exercise.

What Liv saw when she stepped through the Door of Reflection didn't compute at first. She was standing in front of a closed door. Beside her was Clark, and constricting her chest was a white dress. For a long moment, she simply stared down at the strange garment that hung from her body and trailed behind her. Then

Clark held out his arm to her with a pleasant smile on his face. "Are you ready to walk down the aisle?"

"No!" she yelled as she stumbled through the Door of Reflection. Everyone in the Chamber of the Tree stared at her.

CHAPTER FIVE

"Warrior Beaufont," Hester said, her voice shrill. "Are you all right?"

Liv spun around to affirm that she'd stepped all the way through the Door of Reflection. She covered her mouth, mortified that she'd screamed out loud. With a slow nod, she turned back to the council, who were all regarding her with looks of concern.

The Chamber of the Tree was full, with every single Warrior present. To Liv's surprise, standing on Decar's spot was a slender young man with a black mohawk. She studied the council and found another stranger in the place where Adler had sat once. It was a woman of about twenty, her black hair short on one side and long on the other. In her nose was a loop, and many tattoos covered her arms and neck.

Before she could ask any questions, Haro waved her to her spot. "Warrior Beaufont, you've been through quite the ordeal. I'm certain that your consciousness is still processing the death of Adler Sinclair."

"Which you're responsible for," the woman said.

"It's nice to meet you too," Liv said, taking her spot next to Stefan.

"Ms. Beaufont, this is Kayla Sinclair, and beside you is Spencer Sinclair," Bianca said. "They are the last two remaining Sinclairs, cousins of Adler and Decar. I assume you can understand how upsetting it was to find out that their only living relatives were murdered."

"We don't call it 'murdered' when people are stopped who were breaking the law," Liv replied. "It's call justice."

"Regardless of your stance on my relatives' conduct, it was still incredibly traumatic to learn that Adler and Decar were dead," Kayla said.

"Of course it was," Bianca said in a strangely soothing tone. "As it was for me."

"Oh, really," Liv challenged. "Did you know the Sinclair brothers well?"

Kayla shook her head. "You don't have to know a relative to feel the pain of their loss."

"And I'm guessing the council contacted you with the information?" Liv inquired.

Raina shook her head, a scrutinizing expression on her face as she eyed the new Councilor. "No, actually. Kayla and Spencer simply showed up. We were all surprised since we were unaware that there were any remaining Sinclairs."

"How interesting," Liv said, mulling over the strangeness of the new situation.

The white tiger stepped out from the shadows, a similar expression of scrutiny on his face. Liv's back muscles twitched where Jude had attacked her when she was trying to unregister her magic, or at least she had experienced the hallucination that he did.

"If the introductions are over," Lorenzo began, "then I think we better continue with House business. Spencer, are you ready for your first case? If you need more time to adjust, that's understandable."

"Wait, I wasn't given any time to adjust," Liv complained, remembering how Adler had insisted that she train at the same time that she took on cases.

Clark covered the side of his face with his hand, shaking his head.

"Well, it's true," Liv went on, seeing his disapproval. "I was told that the Beaufonts would be replaced in the House if I didn't take on my Warrior responsibilities."

"That's true," Haro said.

"That was simply because you abdicated your role as Warrior and gave up your magic," Bianca said. "I think your loyalty was in question."

"I think," Hester began, "that it was Adler trying to set Warrior Beaufont up for failure. Now that we are aware of his end goals, much of his behavior has been illuminated."

"Regardless of what's happened in the past, I think it's a good idea for Spencer to have time to adjust to his new role," Lorenzo stated. "Maybe he could shadow one of the Warriors. Stefan, for instance." He directed his attention to him, a stern expression in his eyes. "You're working on the elf negotiations. I think that would be a good way for Spencer to learn."

"Actually, I think working solo on this one is for the best," Stefan answered at once.

"And I'm certain that Warriors don't get a vote on such matters," Kayla said.

So being an asshole runs in the Sinclair family, Liv thought.

"Although I'm sure you have the rule book already memorized on your first day," Stefan began, "a Warrior's opinion is taken under advisement. It was only under Adler's dictatorship that absolute rule by the council happened."

"I don't appreciate the disrespectful banter regarding my deceased cousin," Kayla said, sounding hurt.

It was an act. Liv knew it. But it was a waste of her efforts to point it out.

"Warrior Ludwig is correct though," Haro stated. "And I'm sorry to admit that Adler did steamroll us more than once. At times, I wanted to object, but I didn't, and for that, I'm sorry."

"The matter of Spencer's assignment is still up for discussion," Lorenzo said. "I vote that he accompany Stefan. All those in favor."

Four of the council members raised their hands.

"Then it's settled," Lorenzo said victoriously.

Liv wasn't surprised that Haro had voted with Bianca, Kayla, and Lorenzo. He was strategic and probably thought Stefan would be a good trainer for Spencer. Based on the look on Stefan's face, though, he disagreed. Liv knew he liked working alone, unless it was with her.

"And now that brings us to the topic of registering magicians," Clark said. "Or rather, I'd like to propose that we unregister all."

This bold suggestion got every one of the Councilors talking.

"So are you all right?" Stefan asked Liv in a low whisper.

"Yeah, why?"

"Because a minute ago you screamed 'no' when you stepped into the Chamber of the Tree. What did you see in the Door of Reflection? Was it Adler?"

Liv gulped. She didn't want to lie to him. "No, it was something less sinister."

"Not by the sound of your voice," he said. "You seemed really adamant about something."

How could she tell him that she'd had to face her commitment issues in the Door of Reflection without making him worried? Everything was moving too fast for her, and yet, she'd taken her time getting to this place with him. And currently, she had zero regrets about the relationship. Stefan was good for her. As a person, he didn't make her want to puke. And as a man, he was pretty incredible. And as her boyfriend…

Liv couldn't finish the thought right now, so she simply offered him a forced smile. "Are you looking forward to having a newbie Sinclair along for the ride?"

He shook his head. "No, and it's curious that mustache wanted him paired up with me." He indicated to Lorenzo with a small nod of his head.

The council was so engrossed in discussing the topic of unregistering magicians that they took no notice of Liv's and Stefan's conversation.

"Although under Adler's rule, the registration system

was abused, I don't think that's a good reason to think it will happen again," Lorenzo said.

"Abused?" Clark questioned, his face red. "Our parents were killed. Our siblings. This isn't a matter of abuse. This is about murder."

"There is no evidence to prove my cousin did anything," Kayla stated.

"He admitted to it," Liv stated. "And I saw it in a vision."

"I will remind you," Bianca began, "that visions of the past aren't reliable proof of guilt. They are impossible to prove."

Clark sighed loudly. "The point remains that it's wrong for us to force magicians to register their magic. It places too much power in the hands of the council, and until we have checks and balances in place, I don't think we should keep requiring magicians to register. We most certainly shouldn't punish them for not registering, as we've done in the past."

"I would agree with this," Trudy chimed in.

Liv knew the warrior had been conflicted by being assigned to force magicians to register their magic. She'd overlooked the law when she could, and been reprimanded for it by the council. Liv also knew that Trudy was keeping a secret about being a seer, and she could only wonder what visions of the future she'd been given.

"I propose that we table this conversation until the Mortal Seven are found," Lorenzo stated.

"I second that," Hester stated, turning her attention to Liv. "How is that going, by the way?"

"It's going," Liv answered at once, wishing that everyone in the Chamber wasn't staring at her.

The names of the Mortal Seven families were illuminated on the tree trunk behind the council. However, it was only the surnames, with no first names written on the branches, like with the magician families.

"Do you care to expand on that?" Bianca asked.

Liv definitely didn't want to give Miss B the satisfaction of knowing she hadn't made any progress on figuring out how to locate the Mortal Seven or identify which one should become Councilor. She considered telling them about John, but that seemed like only anecdotal evidence at this point. She needed something more concrete.

Her phone rang in her pocket, a loud siren noise she'd never heard it make before.

"Ms. Beaufont, it is common knowledge that cell phones are to be silenced during these meetings," Bianca said.

Liv pulled the phone from her pocket. "It is silenced."

"Apparently it isn't," Kayla said, wearing the same snooty expression as Bianca. Those two were going to get along just fine.

"Oh, I get it," Liv said, reading the caller ID.

"Get what?" Bianca asked, a sharp edge to her voice.

"Who is the only person who can make a phone ring even when it's silenced?" Liv asked, backing toward the exit.

"Who?" Hester asked.

Liv held up her phone. "Father Time. Sorry, guys, but when the boss calls, I've got to take it."

CHAPTER SIX

Liv wasn't sure if she was imagining it, but she could have sworn Kayla's face constricted with tension when she mentioned Father Time. For that reason, she took a more convoluted route to Roya Lane on her way to see Papa Creola, remembering when Adler had followed her.

Of course, Papa Creola wouldn't tell her what he wanted her to do. Instead, he simply said, "Get here now!"

To which she replied, "A please wouldn't kill you."

Apparently, it would have because he hung up on her.

Roya Lane was buzzing with excitement when Liv stepped through the portal. As usual, she got curious looks from passersby. However, unlike usual, the gnomes weren't scowling at her and hiding their illegal wares, the elves weren't pointing, and the fairies weren't covering their mouths as they no doubt gossiped about her. Instead, many of the magical creatures waved to Liv like they were best friends reunited after a long time.

Twice a gnome came up and offered her a somewhat

friendly handshake. An elf even gave her a piece of hemp candy, which she promptly put in the trash bin—not because she didn't accept candy from strangers, but because elf food would make her hallucinate.

"She's the one who stopped Adler Sinclair," she heard someone say as she passed.

"Really shaking things up in the House of Fourteen," someone else said.

"Things aren't going to be the same now that Liv Beaufont woke mortals up," another said.

Liv's chest swelled with pride as the many people on the streets praised her. She hadn't been sure how the information regarding mortals would be received by the other magical races. The council had been working with the different official head offices on a strategy, so she was out of the loop. This reminded her that she probably should have told the council about the meeting with the President of the United States, but it had skipped her mind, with the new Sinclairs randomly showing up.

It took Liv longer than usual, thanks to all those congratulating her, to get to the far side of the lane. She was just about to duck into The Fantastical Armory when something out of the corner of her vision caught her attention. She would have dismissed it and hurried in to see Papa Creola, but the image couldn't be ignored.

King Rudolf Sweetwater was holding a baby doll to his chest and appeared to be trying to breast-feed it as he lovingly combed its plastic head. Liv ducked into a store full of magical nursery items like a teething balm that made all the baby's teeth grow in overnight, making quick work of a usually slow process. There were also cribs that promised to put the baby to sleep, and rattles that silenced a crying baby. Literally, the rattle would make it so the screaming child couldn't make a peep.

"Ummm…what are you doing?" Liv asked, sidling up next to the fae king.

"Shhh," Rudolf said, pressing a finger to his lips. "I've almost got him or her to sleep."

"It's a baby doll," Liv explained. "It doesn't sleep, and I think the pink jumper it's wearing means it's a girl."

"No one ever likes it when you stereotype," Rudolf said, giving her a disgusted look.

"Oh? Well, I don't like it when you use absolutes." Liv pointed at the baby doll. "Again, what are you doing? Are you pretending to breast-feed that thing?"

He threw up the hand holding the doll, letting it dangle in the air. "Very well, Liv wants to talk, so I can't put the baby to bed." Rudolf tossed the doll into a nearby crib and stuck his hands on his hips. "Are you happy now? You've got my full attention, and the baby is going to be up all night. What do you want?"

Liv's eyes widened with shock. "Ooookay. This is not awkward."

Rudolf shook his head, his face softening. "I'm sorry. I'm just so stressed right now with the changes going on with the fae kingdom, my new business ventures, and Serena being pregnant."

"Wait, what?"

"Yeah, it's true. We've launched a line of products and business is booming, but it leaves me little time to just chill, which makes Ruddy a very grumpy fellow."

"First of all, that's not what I was asking about," Liv

began. "Secondly, please don't ever refer to yourself as 'Ruddy.'"

He crossed his arms over his chest and stuck out his bottom lip. "But Rudolf feels better when he talks about himself in the third person."

Liv held up her hands, trying to calm the king, who looked close to throwing a tantrum. She glanced around for some sort of magical item that relaxed children but couldn't find anything in the vicinity.

"Okay, what is this about Serena being pregnant? You two wasted no time."

"Yeah, it's true, which is why I was trying to get good at breastfeeding."

"Ummm, you're not the one who has to feed the baby," Liv explained.

He huffed. "There you go again with that judgmental stereotyping. I guess just because I'm a man, I can't nurse. Is that right?"

"Pretty much. And congrats. How far along is Serena?"

"I don't know, a day or two," Rudolf stated.

Liv arched an eyebrow at him. "Usually you can't find out if someone is pregnant for several weeks."

"Yes, but we've been doing it nonstop."

Liv slammed her hands over her ears and shook her head. "I don't want the details of your sex life."

He gawked at her. "Who said anything about sex?"

"You just did."

"No, I was referring to our secret handshake. Every time we make a deal or do something for the business, we shake on it. I think we've already done it like thirty-five times today. And yesterday was a doozy."

"That's not how babies are made," Liv said.

"Are you sure?" Rudolf asked.

"Yes. You have to have sex to make a baby."

"Oh, well, who has the time for that? With the new ventures and all the kingdom business, little Rudolf has been beat."

Liv's eyes fluttered shut with annoyance. "Ewww."

"So, are you telling me that Serena isn't pregnant?"

"I'm no doctor, but I'm guessing she's not," Liv said.

"Well, that's probably for the best. I don't have the time to nurse a baby right now, not to mention I wasn't looking forward to getting fat."

"Again, you aren't the one... You know what, never mind."

CHAPTER SEVEN

As usual, Liv felt dumber after her interaction with Rudolf. He had a good heart, though, and sometimes that gave her hope that he wouldn't run the kingdom of the fae into the ground.

The Fantastical Armory was empty when she entered. Subner appeared to be busy working on something at the counter. There was a tiny, contained fire in the middle of a smooth, flat stone. The gnome was very focused as he peered into the orange and blue flames.

Cautiously, Liv approached, watching as Subner rotated small objects in his fingers.

"What are you doing?" she asked.

Subner lifted his hand and dropped one of the silver balls she'd given him at Rudolf's wedding into the flames. They were made from metal from the Isle of Man, and held strange properties imbued by the giants. That was as much as she knew.

Unhurriedly, Subner glanced up at her. "Nothing."

"Right, and I'm currently standing on my head."

Not amused, Subner scowled. "No, you're not."

"And you're not doing nothing." He dropped the other silver ball into the flames, watching it intently.

"I'm making something," he finally said.

"And I absolutely don't want to know what it is. I'm not at all curious."

He fanned the fire gently. "That's good."

"So whatever you do, don't tell me."

Subner pointed to the door at his back. "Papa is down in his office."

Liv sighed. "Good, I wanted to walk down a trillion flights of steps."

He lifted his gaze away from the fire. "Are magicians taught that sarcasm is a productive way of communicating?"

"You and the giants don't care for sarcasm much, do you?"

Subner shook his head. "Although it might seem strange to you, Warrior Beaufont, we say only that which we are thinking."

"If you say that much, you little secret-keepers. I swear gnomes and giants went to the same school of tight-lipped privacy."

"I'd contend that this is better than the fae, who over-share," Subner said.

"I can't argue with that," Liv said, her strange conversation with Rudolf still streaming through her head. "Did you know that some fae who will remain nameless think they can reproduce from a handshake?"

Subner glanced up suddenly. "You mean the cheeky monkey? Of course, they can get pregnant from that."

Liv's hand popped to her mouth. "Are you serious?"

Subner's face remained impassive. "Of course, I'm not. Do you see how confusing it is when you say things you don't mean or that are untrue?"

Liv narrowed her eyes at the gnome. "That was a rude trick. And I think you undervalue the fine art of sarcasm. People know when I'm joking."

"Do they?" he questioned.

"Don't you?" she countered.

He shrugged. "Yes, I guess so. But I think calling it an art form might be a bit of a stretch."

She started for the door to the stairs, shaking her head. "True. I get that it's not like the metalwork you're doing there, making silver bullets."

"That's not what I'm doing, actually. I'm…wait, that was a trick."

"No. If it had been a trick, it would have worked. It was a mediocre attempt to trick you," Liv stated.

"Papa Creola is expecting you. You're already late," Subner said dismissively.

"He's the freaking father of time. I think he knows I'm going to be late," Liv exclaimed, rolling her eyes as she pulled open the door.

"He also knows you're going to trip on the third-to-last stair," the gnome said, his attention back on his work.

"I tripped on the first flight of stairs," Liv said, rubbing her ankle.

"So?" Papa Creola asked, sucking on his pipe.

"So, Subner said I'd trip on the third-to-last stair."

"From the top," Papa Creola answered.

"Who talks that way?" Liv questioned, rolling around her ankle. "Wouldn't you just say... You know what, never mind. It's a wonder any of us communicate at all."

"Learning how to communicate despite all our nuances is part of the magic of this world," Papa Creola said with a speculative glint in his eyes.

Liv glanced at the giant hourglass that hung over the fireplace. It had appeared to recover since the mortals had been awoken to magic. However, Liv knew the balance was always shifting. It only took a few small events for time to be in jeopardy.

"Soooo..." Liv began. "I'm thinking of buying a new laptop this afternoon."

"You should wait. Prices will be better this weekend," Papa said casually.

"And there's a new Mexican place in town I'm thinking—"

"You'll get food poisoning. Wait six weeks until they've gotten a different dishwasher."

"And if I play the lottery tonight?" Liv asked.

"Doesn't matter when you play it. A lottery win isn't in any of your futures."

Liv sighed. "See? That wasn't hard. Who says you're an uptight man who is unwilling to help others?"

Papa Creola's face creased into wrinkles.

"No, it was a question," Liv said, trying to recover

from her blunder. "Who is this person that would call you anything of the sort? Not me, for sure. But I'll keep an eye out, and report any misconduct straight to you, boss."

"Speaking of being your boss," Papa began, "I have an important case that needs your immediate attention."

"What is it?" Liv asked, leaning forward in the armchair.

"You're going to have to work fast to solve this one. Again, mortals are in danger."

Liv drew in a breath. "Couldn't you have told me about it a little earlier, and then I wouldn't have such a rushed deadline?"

Papa Creola laid his pipe on the side table and stared into the fire. "Just because I get glimpses of events doesn't mean I see the whole picture. Time isn't linear, and neither are the things that happen."

"Now that my head has exploded, would you like to tell me what's going on?" Liv asked.

"One of my greatest nemeses has returned. I'm not entirely sure how. Someone has awoken him," Papa Creola related.

Liv began to rack her brain. Who was Papa Creola talking about? The Grim Reaper? Mother Nature? Santa Claus? She didn't know.

"I have to admit that things have been going along too well for too long. Most of my enemies are dead or gone, making my job easier." Papa Creola laid his hands over his belly, sighing deeply. "I fear I've gotten complacent. I admit that I didn't see this one coming."

"Who is this great adversary?" Liv asked, nearly falling off her chair.

He let out a long breath. "It's none other than the SandMan."

Liv could have been lightly slapped and fallen off her chair right then. It wouldn't have taken much to throw her off her balance. "Say what?"

"Yes, I know," Papa Creola said, nodding. "He's back. It's terrifying."

"For who?" Liv asked. "Grouchy children who don't want to tuck in early?"

Papa Creola flashed her a disapproving look. "Don't you underestimate him. The SandMan is a horrible being. He'll do things that would make the devil appear ordinary."

"Like put people to sleep so they can snore blissfully for hours? Sounds petrifying," Liv said, thinking of her own predicament of not being able to sleep for more than a few hours at a time.

"No, like put mortals into a slumber so they sleep for ages, not doing anything for the eternity of their lives. They then fade into nothingness, contributing nothing and being nothing."

"Oh, and that *is* a bad thing," Liv said darkly.

"And since the SandMan can only affect mortals, that means that as he puts them all to sleep, magic is compromised."

"Once again, right?" Liv asked.

"Exactly," Papa Creola answered.

"I thought the SandMan was responsible for all of our sleep. If someone just awoke him, which I'll remind you is ironic, then what's the deal?"

"He's only responsible for putting mortals to sleep, but he

doesn't understand limits. He never has. He's always gone too far. Long ago, he helped them sleep when magic kept them awake, but he always made them sleep for days at a time. Then the House came into existence to help balance things, and since then, the SandMan has been out of commission. That sent him into more of a rebellion. He started making mortals sleep for longer, and that was when I had him subdued."

"Wow, so the SandMan lost it, huh?" Liv asked.

"Yep," Papa Creola answered. "He got power-hungry and sent mortals into comas. He's been awoken again, and I fear that means he'll do what he did before. He'll put all mortals to sleep forever."

"And once again, we're right back to where we were before," Liv said, standing suddenly, her ankle resisting her weight as she began to pace.

Papa Creola shared Liv's concern with a single look. "Someone has awoken him. Someone who is powerful, and knows where I hid him long ago. They knew the tune I used to put him to sleep, which is what he must hear to wake."

"Does anyone find it interesting that the man responsible for sleep had to be put into a deep sleep?" Liv asked.

Papa Creola glanced around. "I don't think so."

Liv yawned, strangely tired. "Okay, fine. What do you need me to do?"

"I need you to put him back to sleep."

She gave him a deadpan look. "I love that you're serious."

"I love that you don't even question me at this point," he fired back.

"How do you want me to put the SandMan to sleep?" Liv asked.

"You have to read him a bedtime story," Papa Creola answered.

Liv lowered her chin. Huffed. "Yeah, that seems about right."

CHAPTER EIGHT

Papa Creola explained to Liv that he had changed the incantation that used to awaken and put the SandMan to sleep since someone had apparently figured it out. Instead of a song, it was now a bedtime story. A really long one that took several minutes to read, and the SandMan had to be listening, or it wouldn't work.

Liv felt as though her job had gone from fighting evil to babysitting all of a sudden. The SandMan sounded like an angry toddler who was going to challenge her every step of the way as she tried to get him to sleep.

She sighed her frustration as she entered the official brownie office. Mortimer, as usual, was her go-to for finding the SandMan since Papa Creola, of course, didn't know where he was.

It finally made sense to Liv why the President of the United States had fallen asleep during their meeting, but if the SandMan could affect people in such high positions, that was even more worrisome. Papa Creola had also explained that car accidents and other similar incidents were on the rise. Mortals all over the world were falling asleep at the most inopportune moments, putting their lives and others in danger.

Pricilla was humming as she dusted the light fixtures in the hallway when Liv entered. She flashed her a pleasant smile and raised her finger to her mouth.

"Please be quiet if you can," the secretary encouraged. She pointed to a bassinet in the corner of the reception area. "The baby is asleep."

"Baby?" Liv questioned. "I thought you were just pregnant?"

"Yes, but the gestation period for brownies isn't long," Pricilla explained in a whisper.

Liv nodded, remembering that this was similar for other small mammals like rats and rabbits.

"Mortimer is in the back, in his office," Pricilla said, buzzing around the area, cleaning furiously. That must have been how she'd taken off the baby weight so fast. The place was spotless, even more so than it had been before.

"Thanks," Liv said, tiptoeing down to Mortimer's office.

The Head Official for the Brownies had his head on his desk when Liv ducked into his office, casually clearing her throat to get his attention.

A soft whimper escaped Mortimer's mouth. "I'm sorry. I just can't…"

"Mortimer?" Liv asked, inching closer to the desk. "Are you all right?"

He looked up suddenly, his already large eyes widening. "Warrior Beaufont? It is you. I thought it was Pricilla coming to give me my lunch."

"And that's a problem why?" Liv asked, noticing that the window in his office pictured turbulent seas, which was different from the last time she had been there.

"I can't eat," he said, lacing his fingers together. "I don't have the time."

"But I thought things were easier with the new filing and computer systems," Liv questioned.

"They were, but then the baby came, and now I feel all this pressure."

"From Pricilla?" Liv questioned, trying to take a seat in the small chair.

"Oh, no," Mortimer answered. "She's lovely, taking care of the baby and the administrative work and cleaning the office."

"So what's the problem?" Liv asked, wondering where she could get a Pricilla.

"Isn't it obvious?"

Liv shook her head.

"I've got a family depending on me now, as well as thousands of brownies. And I'm just Mortimer. Sad little Mortimer who is going to disappoint my son and send my family into squalor and let everyone else down."

Liv finally understood. "You're feeling the pressures of parenthood, aren't you?"

"Yes," Mortimer said, putting his head back on the desk and starting to bang it on the wood. "What if I fail my son? What if he hates me? What if he turns into a lazy brownie and it reflects on me?"

Liv sighed. "I'm not a parent, but I think many go through this. Are you close to your parents?"

Mortimer brought his head up, his forehead red from

abuse. "Well, yes. My pops is the best person I know. And my mum, well, she's the hardest worker I have ever seen. Well, besides Cilla. That woman never takes a day off."

Liv smiled. "Don't you see? Your son—"

"Seurat," Mortimer supplied.

"Right, well Seurat is going to look up to you the same way you do to your parents because despite your worries, you're incredible, Mortimer," Liv explained. "You manage tons of brownies. You attracted a woman who I sort of want to be my personal assistant. And you changed your life when you realized it wasn't serving you."

Mortimer thought that over and then nodded. "Yeah, I guess you're right. I'm just worried that I won't be enough for Seurat."

"I think that's precisely what makes you an incredible parent," Liv stated. "If you didn't feel that way, there might be something wrong with you. But you, Mortimer, are always reaching to be better, and for that, I admire the hell out of you."

The brownie beamed. "As usual, you, Warrior Beaufont, have made me feel better while saving the world. Simply amazing."

"Well, I haven't saved the world yet," Liv stated. "There's another problem that once again puts mortals in peril, which means the rest of the world, as usual."

"Not mortals," Mortimer said, covering his mouth.

"Yes, apparently the SandMan has been awoken—"

The brownie gasped, cutting Liv off. She thought she was going to have to explain things to Mortimer, but it appeared, based on his reaction, that he already knew about the SandMan and his potential threat.

"So you need my help locating him, do you?" Mortimer asked, typing wildly on his computer.

"Thank you," Liv answered. "And that's right. I was hoping one of your brownies could help locate him."

"They can, but only if we can determine what his real name is," Mortimer said, his brow furrowing as he studied his monitor. "We need that to find him."

"Oh, well, hold on a sec," Liv said, messaging Papa Creola. There were a few benefits to having Father Time on speed dial, besides that he told her when to buy electronics and avoid Mexican food.

A moment later, a text came back from the gnome.

"Tell the Head Official for the brownies to ask his wife," Papa Creola answered.

Liv rolled her eyes at the reply. This was another of the gnome's games. He was up to something. She just knew it.

Lowering her phone, she blinked at the brownie. "Do you think your lovely receptionist and wife would know the name of the SandMan?"

He gave her a dumbfounded expression. "Well, I'm not sure. I expect it's worth trying."

Pressing a button on a machine beside his keyboard, he said, "Dear, can you—"

"Shhh," Pricilla said in reply. "Please whisper. The baby is sleeping."

"Sorry, dear," Mortimer whispered. "Will you please come here?"

A moment later, the beautifully poised Brownie appeared in the doorway to the office, appearing to still be listening for Seurat in the front office. "Yes, dear?"

"Do you, by chance, know the name of the SandMan?" Mortimer asked his wife.

Her face brightened. "Of course. I once worked for the Navarro family. Thank you, dear, for remembering that. And here I thought I was just your secretary and baby machine."

"Oh, honey. You know that's not true," Mortimer said, giving Liv a sideways look that spoke of his instant gratitude.

Damn it, Papa Creola is a genius, she thought.

"I seem to remember that his name was Zeno Dutillet," Pricilla said, musing on the notion.

Immediately Mortimer began typing. He studied the screen before bringing up a victorious expression.

"Did you find him?" Liv asked, excited that she'd be closing this case so soon.

"No," he said at once. "But I have the information out for the brownies to locate. It won't be long."

"And…" Liv said, glancing at him and his wife.

"And, also I realized that my wife is the smartest brownie in the world," Mortimer said, picking up on the hint.

Pricilla laughed shrilly with excitement, waking the baby immediately. She was so happy that it didn't even seem to bother her. She trotted off to comfort Seurat.

Mortimer bowed his head. "Again, thank you, Warrior Beaufont. You haven't just saved my sanity, but probably my family and my business. Never, ever stop paying me these visits."

"I think our partnership is mutual," Liv said, indicating his computer.

"I hope so," he agreed. "I'll let you know as soon as I hear about Zeno Dutillet's whereabouts. Keep an eye out for a brownie visitor. They will have the information."

CHAPTER NINE

Liv had rushed to her apartment as soon as she'd gotten the message from Sophia. It didn't sound urgent, but there was definitely concern in her voice, although she hadn't expanded on what was wrong. The little magician had only said that she wanted Liv to come home when she could to see something.

When she was almost to her door, she recognized the giant standing out front. However, Rory didn't quite look like himself. He was wearing a Renaissance costume, with his hair pulled back into a small ponytail and…makeup.

Liv halted at the sight of him, tilting her head to the side. "Are you wearing tights?"

"No," he answered, then shook his head. "Yes, I guess that's what they are."

"And is that blush on your cheeks?"

"It's stage makeup," he answered expressionlessly.

"Because?"

He held up his phone, displaying a message from Sophia. "She told you to come here too?"

Liv nodded. "Yes, but don't think you can distract me from my line of questioning. Why do you have on eyeliner?"

"It's for a thing I'm doing," he replied vaguely.

"Does this thing have anything to do with your mysterious occupation?" Liv asked.

He shook his head. "No, this is my outlet. I do this because my job doesn't allow for much creativity."

"I believe that's the most you've told me about your job," Liv said as she stepped around him. "We're going to talk about this get-up you're wearing and why in just a minute. First, let's go check on Soph."

Rory agreed with a nod, following Liv inside. Thankfully, the place appeared to be in order. Liv ran to Sophia's room, calling for her.

"I'm in here," she replied, her voice coming from the bathroom.

Liv gave Rory a hesitant expression, and he immediately halted.

"You go ahead," he stated. "I'll wait out here."

Carefully, Liv slid back the door to the restroom, peeking her head through. "Soph, is everything all right?"

The girl wasn't sick, as she had expected. Instead, she was trying to pull her egg across the marble floor on a small rug. The egg, which Liv had last seen this morning, was strangely bigger.

With a tired sigh, Sophia stood, wiping her hand across her brow. "I'm fine, but I could definitely use some help."

Confused, Liv stepped backward, waving Rory into the bathroom. "It's fine for you to come in."

"What's going on, Soph?" he asked, coming into the

bathroom. His eyes widened at the sight of the egg, which somehow was twice the size it had been that morning. Before, it had been about the size of a football. Now it was more like a beach ball.

"I'm not sure," she said, indicating the dragon egg. "Is it normal for him to grow so fast?"

Rory scratched his head. "I'm not sure. I have limited experience with dragon eggs. Well, with dragons in general, really."

Sophia sighed. "Yeah, I figured. I looked in the book, and it didn't say anything about it."

"Why are you in the bathroom?" Liv asked.

"He says he's cold, and I figured the easiest way to warm him up would be to run him a hot bath," she explained.

"Good idea," Liv said. "But how are you going to get him in and out of the bath?"

"That's one reason I need your help," Sophia answered. "Also, I'm worried that if he keeps growing so fast, we might have to move out."

Liv shook her head. "No way. You're staying with me. It's safe here."

"Soph is right, though," Rory mused. "The dragon might need a place that's more conducive to his growth. They usually prefer it really hot. Dragons often have their eggs under mountains or close to a volcano."

"Well, my little sister isn't moving to a mountain, so we're going to have to figure something else out," Liv said with authority.

"Rory, would you mind helping me, please?" Sophia asked, pointing to the blue egg. "He says he's really cold."

The giant nodded. "I think this is a good sign. He's gone through a growth spurt."

"Oh, do you think he'll hatch soon?" Liv asked, both excited and nervous about the possibility. She wasn't sure she was ready for whatever came next when the dragon hatched. Would Sophia be pulled away by the demands of being a dragon rider? She was still so young.

The little magician shook her head. "No, he says I'm not ready yet."

"Wait, *you're* not ready?" Liv questioned. "He's the one incubating in a shell."

Rory halted before picking the egg up, studying Sophia. "Have you had a growth spurt lately? You look bigger?"

She glanced down at her body and shrugged. "I think so. I did notice that my dress was a bit shorter this morning."

Liv studied her sister, noting that the green and blue paisley dress hit her just above the knee, whereas before it had been closer to her calf.

"Wait, are you saying the dragon had a growth spurt because Sophia did?" Liv inquired.

Rory thought for a moment. "It's possible. They *are* linked. And if he's saying you're not ready, that might mean you need to grow a bit more, Soph."

"But I don't want her to grow up," Liv complained.

The giant turned, giving her a serious expression. "You realize this is inevitable, right?"

"I know, but I want her to remain young and innocent a bit longer," Liv stated.

"And she will, but Sophia's growth is tied to her dragon's egg now," Rory said. "There's not a lot of information on this subject since the Elite guard the information pretty tightly."

"The Elite?" Sophia asked.

"That's the group of dragon riders," Rory explained. "For years, many thought they were gone, but I think they are just laying low. I've been trying to contact them to make them aware of you since you'll be joining them at some point."

Liv wasn't sure how she felt about any of this. She wanted to be happy for her sister, but how could she when it sounded like a strange group would be stealing her away in the future. And dragon riders had the most dangerous roles, protecting magic. How could she not worry about her sister?

"So these Elite," Liv began. "Have they responded?"

Rory shook his head. "But I'm not a dragon rider, so they have no reason to talk to me."

"They sound sort of snobbish," Liv stated.

"Well, they *are* called 'the Elite,'" Rory related.

"True. Maybe Sophia should contact them. Then she can find out if this growth spurt is normal or what to expect," Liv suggested.

"Yes, I think that's a good idea," Rory said, bending over to pick up the egg.

No one else had touched the egg since Sophia magnetized to it besides when Adler stole it. However, if the dragon needed to get warm, Rory was going to have to pick it up. The egg must have been extremely heavy because Rory grunted, struggling to lift it higher than his waist. Liv had seen him pick up boulders, and, well, her. It surprised her that the egg weighed more.

Carefully he laid the egg in the bath, which was already full of steaming-hot water. It bobbed around for a bit before settling into place.

"We are going to have to figure something out, because I'm going to need a shower later, and prefer not to do it with a dragon's egg," Liv said.

"You could try adding another bathroom," Rory suggested. "You've already turned this once-tiny place into a penthouse."

"Yeah, but I'm not really good with plumbing," Liv stated. "The fountain in the atrium is about as good as I could do about adding anything that involved water."

"And it has flooded the living room six times already," Sophia said with a giggle.

"Hey," Liv chirped, folding her arms over her chest.

"Yes, Liv can release all mortals from brainwashing, but she can't magick a simple bathroom," Rory said with a laugh.

"And you're wearing eyeshadow," Liv fired back. "Care to tell us why?"

He sighed. "Because I'm in a play, obviously."

"Why would that be obvious to anyone?" Liv asked.

"Because acting is one of my hobbies," Rory stated.

Liv huffed. "Who are you? I don't even know."

Rory glanced at Sophia. "You knew I was active in the local theater, right?"

Sophia held up her hands. "Oh, no. Leave me out of this one."

Rory strode for the exit. "Come on, Liv. I'll help you add an extra bathroom. Plumbing pulls on elemental magic, which means it will be easier for me to do."

She followed him out of the bathroom. "Not to mention, those tights probably help."

He gave her a sideways look. "How do you figure?"

"I don't know. They tighten up your magic, maybe." Liv was surprised to find Clark standing in the middle of her living room when they exited the bathroom. He had a worried expression on his face, which was typical. In his hands was the *Forgotten Archives*.

"Is there a reason you all were in the bathroom together?" Clark asked.

"Yes, we were doing Rory's makeup," Liv answered. "We can do yours next if you like."

Sophia giggled. "I think you'd look nice with a bit of mascara."

"I don't," Clark said at once. "And I don't have time to play dress-up." He looked Rory up and down, obviously confused by his costume. He didn't seem to know that Rory was active in the theater either.

"What's going on?" the giant asked, pointing to the book in Clark's hands. "Have you found something helpful?"

Clark nodded. "Yes, and it changes absolutely everything."

CHAPTER TEN

"If you wanted our attention, you have it," Liv said, impatiently watching as Clark flipped through the *Forgotten Archives*. The book, much like *Mysterious Creatures*, was huge, although it appeared to be a compact little volume.

"Hold on." Clark held up a single finger as his eyes scanned the page. "I want to find the exact passage so that I get it right."

"But aren't there a thousand pages or more in that book?" Liv asked.

"Probably more like two thousand," Rory stated.

"And we still have a home remodel project to do," Liv said, trying to hurry Clark up.

He huffed and slapped the book shut. "Fine. I think I remember most of what I read. The book is complicated, and the history isn't told in a linear fashion."

"Because time isn't linear, according to Papa Creola," Liv stated.

"Apparently, when the House of Fourteen was created and the Mortal Seven were asked to join," Clark began, "they had hesitation about their roles. They were worried they would be targeted by magicians or other magical creatures who didn't like their rule."

"Smart mortals, since later they were pushed out of the House and brainwashed," Liv stated.

"And they also felt defenseless since they didn't have magic," Clark continued. "So the Magician Seven, led by Bernard Beaufont, decided to give each of the mortals a gift. These gifts were meant to protect the Mortal Seven from attacks by magical creatures who wanted to harm them based on their position. However, there was another purpose. The original Mortal Seven were picked because they were pure enough of heart and thought to uphold justice related to magic. Since mortals don't live as long, the Magician Seven knew they'd need a way to easily replace the mortals on the council. Unlike magicians, who are appointed based on birth order or picked by the highest-ranking council member in the family, there wasn't a system for picking the right person as successor from each family."

This was more complicated than Liv had originally considered. The role of Warrior and Councilor for magicians was full of rules and regulations. It involved all sorts of technicalities and details that families had to observe. For instance, since there were only siblings left in the Beaufont family, the Councilor was the oldest child of odd birth order, and Warriors were the even-numbered.

That meant Clark had taken the role as Councilor, and one day he would choose his and Liv's successors. If he got married, he could appoint his wife as Warrior, or one of his children. Liv, as Warrior, had to respect his decision, as was expected of all decisions the Councilors made. However, things would be different for the Mortal Seven, since there was only one of them and they'd have to be replaced more often due to their shorter lifespan.

"The thing that is stressed in the *Forgotten Archives* is that the Mortal Seven needed to be pure of heart," Clark continued. "Councilors are supposed to interpret the law and assign cases. I always thought we had a huge role, but what I realize now is that the magicians on the council were really there to guide and advise the Mortal Seven. Back in the day, their vote outweighed ours because they were thought to be more objective about magical issues."

"That makes sense," Liv said. "Mortals not having any magic but governing it makes them way more objective than us."

Rory agreed with a nod.

"That's the reason it was important for the right Councilor to be picked from each mortal family," Clark explained.

"And this gift the magicians gave them was supposed to help with determining who was picked?" Rory asked.

"Yes," Clark answered, again flipping through the book.

"So what was the object they gave them?" Liv questioned, irritated that Clark was stalling, trying to find the right page out of two thousand. Hadn't he heard of a bookmark?

"It wasn't an object," Clark corrected. "It was an animal. A chimera, to be exact."

"What?" Rory asked, his mouth falling open. "But they are incredibly rare."

"Yes," Clark stated. "And these were the seven most powerful ones in the world. They are immortal, spelled to bond to the most pure-hearted in each Mortal Seven family, and also charged with protecting that person with their life. When they do pass, the chimera moves on, attaching itself to the next person in the family."

"And that's how the House of Fourteen knew who the next Councilor was," Liv guessed.

"Exactly!" Clark said enthusiastically.

"This does change everything," Liv said suddenly breathless. "So once I track down a family member, I just have to find the person who has a part-lion-goat-serpent following them around. That should be easy."

"It won't be, though," Clark cut in, his face serious.

"Of course, it won't," Liv said dryly. "It never is."

"I believe the chimera would have to have disguised itself, especially once magic was hidden from mortals," Clark explained.

"So you think the chimeras are still out there, attached to the Mortal Seven?" Sophia asked.

"I don't see why not," Clark stated. "But since we haven't heard any reports of chimeras, I think they are disguised as regular pets."

"Pickles!" Liv said triumphantly, thinking of John's terrier.

Clark shook his head, that familiar serious expression back on his face. "I knew you'd go there immediately, but it's important not to get your hopes up. Pickles could be a chimera, which would make John Carraway one of the Mortal Seven. However, he could also just be a dog."

"So how am I going to find out who in each family has the chimera, making them the Councilors for the House of Fourteen?" Liv asked.

Rory ran his hands through his hair, pulling it out of the low ponytail. "I think I can help with that. Or at least, I believe my mum can. She spent a lot of time researching chimeras. She should know the spell for revealing a disguised chimera. All of this makes perfect sense. The chimeras would have all taken on acceptable forms at the time the mortals were spelled, but they would remain locked in those forms until something released them. That would be for their safety as well as their master's. The spell for releasing them is ancient, but if anyone knows what it is, it will be my mum."

"Well, Shakespeare, lead the way to Bermuda," Liv said, holding out her hand. "I'm sure she can't wait to see me since I'm her favorite person."

"Okay, but don't mention anything about the play," he said, twirling his finger and changing before their eyes into his regular clothes. His makeup disappeared, and his hair returned to its normal wild and curly appearance.

"Because?" Liv asked.

"Because she thinks it's a waste of my talents, and I should be devoting my time to other things," Rory related bitterly.

"Like your daily yoga practice?" Liv asked, making Sophia giggle.

"She doesn't know about that either," Rory said, making for the door.

"How about your knitting hobby?" Liv continued, following him.

"Nope," he answered.

Liv glanced over her shoulder at her siblings. "Oh, the material for blackmail just keeps adding up."

CHAPTER ELEVEN

"Why did you have me portal us to the fae kingdom?" Liv asked, taking three steps to each of Rory's to keep up with him.

"Because," he said.

"That's not really an answer," she stated. "That's the beginning of an answer. And I just saw Rudolf, and my brain cells are still recovering from the experience."

Rory halted and looked down at her. "I'm taking you to see my mum."

Liv glanced around at the flashy slot machines in the Cosmopolitan Hotel and Casino in Las Vegas. "What is your mum doing here?" A moment later, she lowered her voice. "Oh, is she getting into some Sin City business?"

Rory rolled his eyes. "No. And I don't even know what that could possibly mean."

"I don't either, but that's because I'm a good kid."

"You're not either," he said, striding forward again. "And Mum is here helping Serena with something or another."

Liv couldn't help but notice that his face had flushed

pink. "Something or another, huh? Sounds juicy. What is it? And before you say you don't know, I can already tell that you do. Lying will only make me more annoying."

"I don't see how that's possible," Rory told her dryly.

"Ha-ha. So, what's this something or another?" Liv inquired.

"You have to ask them," Rory said firmly. "I refuse to speak on such matters. I just happened to overhear a conversation on a topic I knew Mum was well versed in, and I recommended her to help. She's here now doing just that. End of story."

"And you overheard this conversation about something or another when you were helping King Dumbface with his business ventures, right?" Liv asked.

"Yes, that's correct."

"And that's because you specialize in marketing, right?"

Rory shook his head. "No, Liv. I'm not telling you what I do for a living."

Liv sped up and halted just in front of Rory, making him nearly plow her over. "Why?" she asked with her hands on her hips. "Why is it that most know what you do? I mean, Rudolf doesn't even have a good understanding of the English language, and he knows. And Serena, well, she can't tie her shoes on her own, but *she* knows. But me, the person who has been there for you since the very beginning—"

Rory lowered his chin, giving her a challenging look.

"Okay, I've been there for you for several months, but that doesn't sound as good. Anyway, what's the deal, Rory? Why are you so secretive with me?"

A rare smile flicked to his mouth before he strode

around her. "Because it's funny."

Liv grunted in frustration and hurried after the giant. "Seriously. This is your idea of a joke? You really should take lessons in humor from me. I'm hilarious."

"Hilarious? Really? And Rudolf is the one who doesn't understand the English language?" Rory questioned.

Liv rolled her eyes this time. "Oh, you're so funny. But seriously, you should tell me what you do. I want to know. I thought we were friends."

"We are," Rory said.

"Then why won't you share that part of your life with me?" Liv asked.

He shrugged. "It's more fun this way. Believe me, one day you'll find out the truth, and you'll wish we were still playing this game."

"Oh, so it's something you're not excited about?" Liv observed.

Again, Rory halted, glaring down at Liv. "And you think I perform in local theater and bake on the weekends and do yoga in the evening because I'm fulfilled by my occupation?"

Liv was momentarily speechless. She suddenly saw Rory differently. He did have a lot of hobbies, and maybe that was because whatever he did professionally wasn't fulfilling for him. Or maybe it was because he needed a girlfriend? Or both. There was that giant who worked at the barbeque place in Texas she'd been meaning to "accidentally" have her and Rory run into. Matilda was her name, and she would be great for Rory if he'd loosen up a bit and just be himself. Apparently, she'd have to have him work through some occupational stuff first, though.

"So you don't like your job?" Liv said slowly.

He shrugged. "I mean, I guess. It is a family business that I inherited."

"Wait, I thought you inherited sword-making. There was also a family business? Is it separate from sword-making?"

"Just because we're giants, it doesn't mean we just make swords and dance around bonfires," Rory said with a sigh.

"Wait, you dance around bonfires?" Liv questioned.

He shook his head. "My point is that giants are professionals too. Or at least they can be. I inherited my business from my father. And although it isn't really my interests, it pays the bills."

"You mean that it pays other people's bills," Liv corrected. "I know you send all your money out to take care of the homeless and disadvantaged."

"I don't either."

"Are you really going to lie to me? You're better than that, Rory."

"I'm not lying. I simply don't send *all* my money out."

Liv huffed. "Oh, fine. You're talking semantics now. You send *most* of your money to charities. I'm sure you keep some so that you can buy wood for your bonfires."

He shook his head, giving her an annoyed look. "Let's not talk about this right now. Mum doesn't need to know about my job dissatisfaction."

Liv paused at the elevator, waiting with a large crowd of people. "Seriously, how many secrets do you keep from your mum?"

He glared at her in reply.

"Are you afraid that she's not going to accept you if she

knows you don't love the family business and do love being a thespian?"

"You have met my mum, Liv."

"And I know her to be a very tolerant and accepting person." Liv couldn't finish the sentence without breaking into a chuckle. "Okay, fine. I get it. Your mum isn't the most understanding person."

"She has been pestering me to tell her where you live so that she can break into your house while you're asleep," Rory stated.

"Really? Why? So she can take me out?" Liv asked.

"So she can brush your hair."

Liv laughed, messing up her hair even more as they boarded the elevator. She was the last person to step into the compartment, having to really squeeze in tight for Rory to fit. She pressed the button for the top floor, where Rudolf resided. This superseded all the other floors, making those buttons dim. When the doors closed, Liv turned around to the silent crowd of people. "Thank you all for joining me here."

All of the people on the elevator, many of them drunk, gave Liv questioning expressions. Rory, who had seen her do this a time or two, simply rolled his eyes and glared at the ceiling. "We have a very important mission. Everything is depending on us."

The doors to the elevator opened at Liv's back. She took a single step backward, stepping onto the top floor. "Please await further information. I'll be in touch."

Rory got off the elevator just as the doors closed, everyone on board still giving her curious stares.

CHAPTER TWELVE

"That joke never gets old," Liv said, still giggling from the elevator incident.

"It doesn't for you," Rory said dryly.

"Oh, come on. How can you get on a crowded elevator and not mess with strangers?" Liv asked.

"I simply do." Rory opened the large door to Rudolf's chamber, waving Liv through first.

She halted after stepping through, confusion suddenly crowding her brain. "Ummm…what's going on here?"

Serena was lying on the ground, her arms and legs extended. A circle had been drawn around her, and there were various objects inside it. Bermuda stood to one side, reading from a book. Rudolf was sitting on a large bean-bag, fingers tapping his chin like he was thinking, which was unlikely, Liv thought. He must have simply been in his usual daze.

"I'm doing a fertility ritual," Bermuda explained, her attention on the book.

"Oh, that's the something or other?" Liv asked, looking at Rory. He nodded in reply.

"I didn't realize you two were having issues," Liv stated. "Rudolf, weren't you just confused about how babies are made?"

"I still contend that a fancy handshake can get someone pregnant. My mother told me that was how I came about," Rudolf said.

"I think you misheard her," Liv corrected.

"I didn't. I remember what she said exactly," he argued. "She said, Rudolfus Sweetwater, I made a deal with the devil when I had you. We shook on it, and then you were born, and I've been paying the price ever since."

"I stand corrected," Liv stated. "You misunderstood her, but whatever."

"And even if handshakes would work, Serena would need extra help to get pregnant," Bermuda explained. "It is very difficult for mortals and fae to breed. If it was easy, the population would have doubled long ago since most fae take advantage of mortals' attraction to them."

"So you have to do some sort of pagan ritual to help them have a baby?" Liv asked.

"It's not a pagan ritual, dear Liv," Bermuda corrected. "And what's wrong with your hair? It looks extra messy. Did you just fight a dragon, or were you in a tornado?"

Liv smiled. "I thought you'd like my new do."

"I don't," Bermuda said, returning her attention to the book in her hands.

Liv strolled over and leaned close to the giant. "How much can I offer you to not do this fertility thing right?"

Bermuda shook her head. "They may be dumb as rocks,

but if they want to have a child, so be it. I'm not one of those bigots who think the races shouldn't mix."

Liv thought of Emilio Mantovani, who was apparently in love with a fae. However, his witch of a sister, Bianca, was firmly against the union and had forbidden him to see the girl. It was something Liv wanted to intervene on, but it was none of her business. That excuse was probably only going to hold her off for a bit longer, though.

"Yeah, I guess you're right," Liv said.

"And you wouldn't understand," Rudolf said, leaning back on his beanbag. "It's not like you and Stefan have to worry about interracial problems."

Bermuda looked up suddenly. "What do you mean, 'you and Stefan?' You two aren't having a love affair, are you?"

Liv grimaced. "Do you have to refer to it that way? And yes, we're in a relationship, I guess."

"Liv and Stefan sitting in a tree…" Rudolf began.

Bermuda shut the book, shaking her head. "Well, you're going to have to break things off."

Liv's gaze darted to Rory and back to his mum. "Why? Do you not approve of him? I mean, that would be pretty much par for the course for you."

"It's not about who I approve of," Bermuda began, "although I think he's a bit too goth with his all-black clothing. And he apparently never learned how to brush his hair, about like you. However, it's a matter of law."

"Wait, there's a law that I can't be with Stefan?" Liv asked. "Why?"

Bermuda gave her son an annoyed look. "She doesn't ever read books, does she?"

Rory's face remained impassive. He obviously didn't want to get mixed up in this argument.

"If you had read the laws for the House of Fourteen, you'd know the families are forbidden from entering into romantic relationships with one another," Bermuda explained.

"Really? Why?" Liv asked.

"Isn't it obvious?" Bermuda asked. "If the families bred, there would be issues with lineages, not to mention that it creates objectivity issues. There would be favoritism among Councilors and Warriors. And then there's the matter of representation. If you two have a child, are they to represent the Beaufonts or the Ludwigs? No, relationships among the families muddy everything, and are not allowed."

"So House law dictates who I can date?" Liv asked, her chest starting to ache suddenly.

"Of course." Bermuda opened the book back up. "I advise you to break things off before anyone else finds out about it. Disobeying these laws could cause you both to lose your positions as Warriors."

"But we can't," Liv argued, her heart hammering like a drum. "He's the only eligible Ludwig, and I'm the only Beaufont who can fill the role. If we aren't Warriors, our families will be replaced in the House of Fourteen."

"Then you see how important it is that you end things," Bermuda stated, her attention back on the book. "And really, child, you should have known this. There can be no fraternizing between families of the House of Fourteen."

"But my parents were married and were Councilor and Warrior," Liv argued.

"Yes, but they were appointed to their roles after they were married, which is perfectly acceptable. However, families shouldn't mix. Bloodlines, like I said."

"But it's not like we're thinking of starting a family," Liv stated. "I don't even like to see him every day. It ruins our thing."

"Breeding is the ultimate result of two people being in a romantic relationship," Bermuda explained. "That's why House Royals also aren't allowed to be with other races. Now, why did you come here and interrupt our fertility ritual?"

Liv had suddenly forgotten why she was there. She'd tried to downplay her relationship with Stefan, telling herself it wasn't that big a deal, but the truth was staring her straight in the face now. She loved him, and she couldn't have him. It swiftly broke her heart.

"It's about chimera," Rory said, sensing that Liv needed some help. "We've discovered that the Mortal Seven are each guarded by a chimera, which is disguised as an acceptable animal of some kind. Liv was hoping you could tell her how to unlock them, making them take their natural form."

"Oh, that's quite intriguing," Bermuda stated.

"Can you help me?" Liv asked, her tone morose. She meant with the chimera, but part of her also meant with Stefan. How could she tell him this? It would hurt him. It was hurting her. Things would be very difficult for both of them.

"I'm afraid I can't," Bermuda answered.

Liv's self-pity was enough to overwhelm her right then.

"However," Bermuda continued, "I think I know

someone who can." The giant took off for the door. Liv went to follow her, but Bermuda stopped her. "Stay here, Liv. I'll go and get the information from this person and be right back."

Liv nodded, feeling suddenly lost.

Rudolf waved her over. "Why don't you come over here and help me pick out baby names?"

Reluctantly, Liv dragged herself over to the fae lounging on the beanbag. Serena looked to have fallen asleep on the floor. Rory had taken a place at one of the desks set up toward the back and was inputting numbers into a calculator and studying a report.

"Why are you already picking out baby names?" Liv asked. "Aren't you getting a little ahead of yourself?"

"Nope, I'm planning for the inevitable. That's how the pros do it," Rudolf stated. "Now, we've already picked out the first name for our firstborn son. I'm working on the middle name right now."

"Okay, what do you have so far?" Liv asked.

"There are three options," Rudolf began. "Either Long John Silver, Jack Sparrow, or Christopher Columbus."

"Oh, God," Liv said, shaking her head.

"Oh, yes," Rudolf stated triumphantly. "I bet you can't guess what the first name is going to be."

"I bet I can," Liv said darkly. "You're really going to name a child 'Captain?'"

Rudolf's mouth popped open. "How did you know?"

"Wild hunch," she answered.

"Well, it's a pretty brilliant idea, isn't it?" Rudolf asked.

"It's an idea, for sure," Liv stated. "Are you sure about this baby thing? Maybe you want to wait until you're more used to your role as king and you've matured. Like in a few decades or so?"

Rudolf shook his head. "Serena doesn't have that long. And I'm ready. I think you just know when it's the right time to have a child, and I'm certain that it's now. Or now. Or maybe right now. You get the point?"

"Unfortunately, I do," Liv said, glancing at the door as Bermuda strolled back into the room.

She handed Liv a piece of parchment. "That's got the name and whereabouts of a magician by the name of Rooster."

"Please tell me he's not a chicken," Liv stated. "I am sort of done doing missions with poultry."

"No, he's not a chicken," Bermuda assured her. "However, he's not really a man anymore."

Liv's gaze swiveled to the ceiling. "Of course, he's not, because you can't just send me to a normal person for this."

"Rooster is a shell of a man who endured a devastating heartbreak," Bermuda explained.

"I can strangely relate," Liv said dully.

"He's not going to want to help you, though," Bermuda went on.

"I would expect nothing less."

"And getting to his castle will be very dangerous."

Liv nodded. "Of course, it will be."

"But if you successfully get up there and find a way to fix him, he might give you the incantation for releasing a chimera," Bermuda said.

With a heavy sigh, Liv slipped the parchment into her cape. Going on this impossible mission somehow seemed easier than what she had to do next.

CHAPTER THIRTEEN

The silence that continued to stretch between Liv and Stefan made her insides ache. He hadn't said anything since she'd quit talking over two minutes earlier. His bright blue eyes had dulled immediately upon hearing what she'd learned from Bermuda.

It was almost worse that he wouldn't look at her. Instead, he remained motionless, peering over the side of the skyscraper where they stood looking down on Los Angeles. What was supposed to be an adventurous getaway for the two of them had turned instantly melancholy.

At first, Liv had told herself she could wait to tell him the news. Let them have one last carefree afternoon together. She wanted to pretend this wasn't the end of them, if only for a moment. She wanted to fool herself into believing she could forget what had to happen.

However, when he smiled at her as she stepped through the portal onto the rooftop of the building, she realized she couldn't withhold the truth from him. Stefan had opened his arms to her the way he had been doing lately, his unyielding love for her evident in his gaze. And it crippled her resolve to stall the breakup.

She couldn't pretend her heart wasn't broken. And in truth, she was not going to be able to fool Stefan anyway. He knew something was wrong upon looking at her after she stepped through the portal.

When he dropped his arms and his smile faded, she began to crumble inside. Liv had been so strong all her life. She'd picked herself up after her parents' untimely death. She'd faced challenges she'd never imagined after her siblings died. But somehow she'd opened herself up, allowing herself to fall for Stefan Ludwig. But now, she reminded herself why she'd walled off her heart for so long.

"What's wrong?" he asked after reading the expression on her face.

Those two words.

They cut her deep.

They reminded her that even if she did everything right, something would still be wrong in her life.

Another minute passed before Stefan opened his mouth like he was finally going to respond to the news that they couldn't be together.

Liv focused on him, noticing how his jaw flexed. How his hands brushed through his hair. How he remained staring far into the distance.

She expected him to say something, but instead, he closed his mouth and moved his chin so she couldn't see his face anymore.

"Stefan," she finally said.

"What do you want me to say, Liv?" he asked.

"I don't know," she replied. If he fought her on this, it would only make it harder. If he walked away without showing remorse, she'd regret everything. There was no right thing to say. No matter what, this was going to suck.

"There's no way around this, is there?" he asked.

She shook her head, having spent the entire last few hours trying to find a loophole. "You're the only eligible Ludwig to be Warrior. I'm the only Beaufont. In a different world, at a different time, we could figure something out. I could step down, and you—"

"I would never allow you to do that," he said, spinning to face her directly, the heartache on his face almost too much to bear.

"I know, but if we didn't have to worry about losing our positions, it wouldn't be as big a deal," Liv made herself continue.

"But that isn't our reality," Stefan said. "Families aren't allowed to date. Warriors are forbidden from having relationships."

Liv nodded. "It actually makes sense now, but I don't know why I didn't see it coming."

"Hopefully, because you didn't want to," Stefan said, and then he did the one thing she wanted and didn't want at the same time.

He reached across what felt like a million miles and took her hand. "I'm sorry, Liv."

"I am, too," she said, feeling breathless as the warmth in his hands took over her being.

"I'm sorry I made you fall for me, not realizing that it would never work."

Liv's eyes jerked up from their focal point, a murderous

glare on her face. "Hey, that's not what happened here. I didn't fall."

"You did," he teased in the way only Stefan Ludwig could. "You fell hard."

"You did," she fired back, in disbelief that he'd made her suddenly smile when she'd been so close to tears. Only Stefan…

"Oh, I'm not denying that," he said, pulling his hand from hers. He swept his arm wide at the view. "I felt like someone threw me off this skyscraper. The moment I met you, I knew I'd never met anyone quite like Olivia Beaufont."

"My name is—"

"Liv Beaufont," he said, impersonating her tone. "And I freaking love you, Liv Beaufont. I'm in love with you! Which is why I'm not letting you get away."

"B-b-but Stefan," Liv said, not sure which part to respond to first. He loved her. Of course, he loved her. It was obvious. She'd freaking loved Stefan Ludwig since that first moment he'd showed up to the All Hallows Eve party dressed as F. Scott Fitzgerald and said that real men should be judged on how they treat others rather than appearances. And then he'd continued to secretly steal her heart as he battled demons, both real ones and the ones inside him.

She closed her eyes for a half-beat. When she opened them, he was still regarding her with a confident expression. One that gave her hope. "Okay, so what do we do?" she asked him.

The smile that flicked to his mouth reminded her of his grace.

"We do what we do best as Warriors," he began. "We fight this. We change the laws. We don't settle until justice prevails."

Liv couldn't believe she was suddenly laughing. "Oh, and you think you and I being together is about justice?"

In the way only Stefan could do, he moved around her, blurring with speed and grace. He was at her back, his hand in hers. He twirled her, the city around them streaking in her vision.

When Liv halted in front of him, he was smiling down at her, a genuine grin. Not at all forced. "Only in an unjust world would we not be together, if that was what we wanted."

"Well, and our jobs are to make the world a better place," Liv said, struggling to keep herself from laughing.

Rapidly, like the way he moved, gifted by the grace of a demon, Stefan softened. "You make my world a better place, and I'm not going to just accept this."

"So what do we do?" Liv asked.

"Well, I have a dumb Sinclair shadowing me and a deadline looming for the elf negotiations," Stefan began. "And you've got the huge task of finding the Mortal Seven. But in between saving other people's world, I think we can save our own."

She believed him. And Liv freaking loved that his priorities matched hers. Stefan Ludwig wasn't perfect, but he was perfect for her, or as close as she would get.

"How do you propose we go about doing this?" Liv asked.

He shook his head. "I don't know. You're the one who

knows how to change history and fix problems most don't even know exist."

"Fine," Liv said with a sigh. "I'll have Clark look into House law. I think most of those books were lost, thanks to Adler. Hopefully, they've been recovered now."

"I can have Raina help too," Stefan stated.

"But in the meantime," Liv began, "I think we have to be careful. Before the law changes, we can't risk losing our positions."

Stefan took what felt like a giant step backward. "Yes, unfortunately, I agree."

Liv took her own step backward. "I guess I should let you go then."

"Not if I'm letting you go first."

She gave him a punishing scowl.

"But in all seriousness," Stefan said, making up the space they'd put between one another. "I've never failed a mission, and neither have you. We won't fail to change the law on this one because nothing has ever meant more to me."

Liv couldn't help the smile that spread across her mouth. She had been ready to give up. To settle for heartbreak. But Stefan had given her hope. He had fought back in exactly the right way, and now she couldn't believe she would have ever walked away from this.

"You really want to kiss me right now," he said, a hint of mischief in his voice.

"Not as much as you want to kiss me," she fired back.

He winked. "I refuse to argue with you on this one, Warrior Beaufont."

In a flash, his lips grazed her cheek, then he sped off,

flying over the side of the building, jumping the distance across the wide alley to the next rooftop. Stefan continued to race away, gracefully jumping between buildings until he was out of sight.

Liv shook her head, smiling widely. "What a showoff."

CHAPTER FOURTEEN

The instructions Bermuda had given Liv to find Rooster sounded entirely too easy. She was immediately suspicious. The piece of parchment simply said, "Go to the summit of Mount McLoughlin."

Did the troubled magician have a cabin at the top of the mountain, like how Adler had on the Matterhorn? Liv decided not to stall anymore and created a portal to the summit. She was relieved to see that the portal actually worked, unlike on the Matterhorn, which required walking.

Liv stepped through the portal onto the summit of Mount McLoughlin. It was a clear day in Southern Oregon, not a cloud in the blue sky. From the top of the mountain, Liv could see for miles in all directions.

Some mortals were hiking up to the summit, and many more were already at the top. Liv decided it would be best to cloak herself so she didn't draw unnecessary attention. Clark had given her an update on mortals. They were seeing magic for the first time, and it was more than confusing for them. Currently, the council, governments worldwide, and many diplomats from other magical races were working together to make a global announcement.

Mortals, understandably, didn't know what was happening and would need time to acclimate. Liv was grateful that her job wasn't to explain these bizarre circumstances to them. She wasn't sure how she'd take it if one day she found out that what most thought were fairytales were actually real. Mortals would soon learn that hippies were actually elves, hummingbirds were actually fairies, and moose were actually centaurs.

Liv reminded herself that she had the seemingly impossible task of locating the Mortal Seven, but first, she had to find out how to release the chimeras so she could identify the right person from each family.

Staring at the views from the summit, Liv tried to figure out where this Rooster fellow could be. There wasn't any structure she could see, but that didn't mean one didn't exist.

She unfolded the piece of parchment, hoping she'd missed something. She hadn't. Bermuda had only included the one sentence for directions.

Liv sighed, and to her astonishment, another sentence appeared under the first. It read, "Now create clouds."

"Of course," Liv muttered. Bermuda couldn't have told her all this in advance. Instead, she had to be mysterious and piecemeal the instructions. Liv was sure she was having a good laugh about the whole thing now.

She twirled her hand and puffy white clouds sprang up

all around her, making many of the hikers exclaim in surprise.

The clouds obstructed the view, and also coated Liv in cold dampness. At over nine thousand feet in the air, Liv was in cloud territory.

She glanced around, wondering what the purpose of the cloud coverage was. Looking back down at the parchment, she waited for what she expected to be another set of instructions from the clever Bermuda.

"Turn to the north."

Liv nodded, grateful she was able to finally anticipate how the tricky giant worked. Using her internal compass, fueled by magic, she found north. She was standing on a large flat stone, with many more spread out around her. However, she was only fifteen feet from the edge.

"Now what?" Liv asked, peering down at the magic parchment.

The next set of words appeared on the paper. "Walk off the side of the mountain."

Liv's laughter echoed around her. "So this is how Bermuda is going to off me."

More words appeared on the parchment. "I'm not trying to kill you, Liv."

She laughed again. "Sure you aren't, Bermuda."

"You can call me Mrs. Laurens."

Liv scowled at the parchment. "How did that woman know I'd call her Bermuda right then?"

"Because you're predictable."

Liv rolled her eyes.

"Quit stalling and step off the side of the mountain," Bermuda's words read.

Liv had learned how to float when she'd crossed the lava in Hawaii. She decided it was probably a good idea to cast that spell again, just in case Bermuda was trying to get rid of her.

"It won't work if you're floating," Plato said, appearing next to Liv.

She glared down at him. "Seriously, would you get out of my brain?"

"If you really want me to," he agreed.

She shook her head. "No, it's probably better this way. And what won't work if I use the floating spell?"

"The next part," he said, intentionally not being helpful.

"So you think it's safe to follow Bermuda's instructions?" Liv asked.

"Well," Plato began, "I get that you annoy her, but so do breathing and cool breezes and pretty much everything else, so I wouldn't take it personally. And no, I don't think she'd ever really put you in danger. Well, not into anything you couldn't survive. I think if she was being roasted over a fire, she might even admit to liking you a tiny bit."

"Fine," Liv said, stepping all the way to the edge. Her toes hung over, but thankfully she couldn't see all the way to the bottom because of the clouds. Being on a mountain and potentially falling from it brought sorrow to her stomach, causing her to think of her parents' untimely death. She shook this off, knowing she couldn't focus on that right then.

Closing her eyes, she lifted her foot and took a step forward. To her surprise, her boot met a firm surface. Liv opened her eyes to find she was standing on a cloud. Or so it seemed.

"Now what?" Liv asked.

"Check the parchment," Plato encouraged, still right beside her.

More words scrawled across the paper. "Keep going up."

"Up," Liv said, realization dawning on her. "It's an invisible staircase." Now that she knew what she was looking for, she noticed that the clouds made it a bit easier to make out the direction of the staircase, which didn't go straight up all the way. They arced around, leading to a platform several stories up.

Taking a deep breath, Liv followed the staircase, careful to ensure she was on it at all times and not about to step off into really thin air.

Something occurred to Liv right then. "Hey, did you know the law about Royals not being able to date?"

Plato followed her, climbing from step to step. "Maybe."

"And you didn't think you should tell me?" Liv asked him.

"Well, if I had, you would have stayed away from Stefan, wouldn't you?"

She thought about this for a moment. "So, you didn't tell me so I'd fall for him and then have to do this whole change-the-law business?"

"I think that's a lot of assumptions on your part," Plato said.

"Yes, but I know how you and Father Time and Bermuda manipulate things so that I'll follow your paths," Liv stated.

"I don't know what you mean," Plato said innocently.

"I've never given you mysterious instructions that lead to a castle in the sky."

Liv halted, staring up at the strange structure ahead. "That's a castle?"

Plato's head dropped. "Did I say castle? I meant pirate ship."

Liv shook her head. "Nice try, but you slipped. I caught you. Maybe you're off your game."

"Yeah, maybe."

"Hey, are you going to tell me that one thing you weren't going to tell me on top of the Matterhorn?" Liv asked

"I wasn't planning on it," he answered.

"Oh. Well, when should I expect to learn that secret of yours?"

"Relatively soon."

"When you use the word 'relatively,' it makes me think it might not be very soon."

"Yeah, you're probably right. I'll tell you in between a week and ten years."

"Thanks, pal," Liv said, taking what she instinctively knew to be the last stair. When both her feet were firmly planted, a snow-covered castle appeared before her. The tall spires stretched up past the clouds, peeking out the top. Dead trees and rose bushes lined the castle, and before her was a long rope bridge.

Liv glanced down at the parchment as the next set of instructions appeared.

"The bridge most likely won't survive your crossing."

Liv scowled at the piece of paper. "Are you calling me fat, Bermuda?"

"No," the giant replied somehow.

Taking a step closer to the bridge, Liv dared to look down. Somehow, flowing under the bridge in the sky was a river of molten lava.

"Of course," she said bitterly.

CHAPTER FIFTEEN

"Well, maybe I don't have to cross the bridge," Liv reasoned. "Maybe I can just float across like I did before when crossing molten lava."

"I don't think that will work," Plato said, indicating a sign on the side of the bridge that read, Only those who cross the bridge can enter.

"Seriously, the timing on these messages is starting to get ridiculous," Liv said.

She took a cautious step forward, hoping to test the strength of the rope bridge. Her foot firmly planted on the first rung. It felt surprisingly sturdy.

Holding onto the rope at waist height, Liv took another careful step. Again, the bridge seemed very stable.

"Maybe this won't be so bad," Liv said over her shoulder to Plato.

"Uh-oh," he replied.

"What do you mean, 'uh-oh'?" she asked.

"You had to go and say that."

"Oh, please tell me you don't believe in that jinx stuff?"

"It's not just 'stuff.' It's a law of the universe," Plato explained. "Phrases like 'this isn't so bad' or 'this will be a piece of cake' inevitably bring bad luck."

"You're ridiculous," Liv said, taking another step. She nearly bit her tongue when on her next step, her foot went through the rung, making her lose her balance. The pieces of the broken board fell, landing in the molten lava and burning up instantly. Liv felt the heat rising from the lava, melting the bottom of her boot. She pulled herself up and took a step backward to the prior rung, which she knew to be safe.

"Don't say a word, Plato," she warned, casting a punishing look over her shoulder.

"About what?" he teased. "About how I'm right? Or about how you almost fell to your death? Or about how your hair looks an absolute mess now?"

"I think you know," Liv said, studying the path ahead. There were at least twenty more steps to cross. Some of the boards appeared firm, like the one she was standing on. However, others were splintered and didn't appear to be able to hold her weight.

"I wonder if I can reinforce the bridge using a repair spell?" Liv said, flicking her hand at the boards ahead. She nearly toppled over as the bridge shook violently. The boards that were splintered broke in two and fell into the lava below. The others seemed to age a hundred years before her eyes.

"Probably not a good time to point out that that was a bad idea," Plato said, still standing on the bank behind her.

"No, it was a great time." Liv's tone was overflowing with sarcasm as her balance began to shift from the unsteady boards holding the rope together.

The ropes in her hands shook as she swayed. The bridge felt seconds away from flipping over, and there was little to save her from falling into the lava in the sky.

That was when the simplest yet still revolutionary idea occurred to her. "Lava can't flow in the sky."

"And a castle can't hover above a mountain," Plato added. "What's your point?"

"My point is that this is all an illusion. It's not real," Liv stated with confidence. She hovered her foot above the next step, where the board was missing.

"Are you sure you want to do that?" Plato asked.

"No, I'd rather be playing video games with Sophia and eating Spicy Hot Doritos, but since that's not an option presently, I'll try this."

"Maybe Rooster has Doritos," Plato suggested.

Liv glanced up at the snow-covered castle, realizing that it probably wasn't a castle at all. It might have been a hovel built into the side of Mount McLoughlin for all she knew. Rooster had to be an incredibly powerful magician to surround his home with such strong illusions.

"I don't think he's the type to stock junk food," Liv said, realizing she was stalling. "And I doubt that he has video games, either."

"Whenever you're done stalling, I'm interested to see if your theory about the illusions holds up."

"Seriously Plato, it's creepy how much you're in my head lately," Liv said, drawing a breath.

"You think that's creepy, but you're the one who won't get rid of the spiders living in the apartment," Plato fired back.

"They aren't doing any harm," Liv argued.

"But you think of them as roommates."

"I do not," Liv stated flatly.

"Then why did you name three of them Phoebe, Monica, and Rachel?" Plato asked.

"Seriously, Plato, my head is already crowded enough without you in there."

"Yes, your head is a cramped and dark place. I can attest to that."

Liv tried to shake off the ridiculous conversation and focus on taking the next step. "It's not real. The lava isn't real. The bridge isn't real. It's just a path."

She could hear her heart beating in her ears. If she was wrong, then this would be how she'd die. There would be no time to recover and cast a spell before she tumbled to her death, and Plato probably wouldn't be able to save her. The lava was too close and the fall too short.

"There is no lava," Liv repeated to herself. She held her breath as she let her foot come down. It hit something solid.

Jerking her head down, Liv noticed that she was standing on what appeared to be nothing. She was walking on thin air. Yet again.

"Far out," she said in a hushed voice.

"Yes, very good," Plato commended. "There also isn't a spoon."

Her chest suddenly abounding with adrenaline, Liv

shook her head. "Oh, shush it, Plato. You knew this all along, didn't you?"

He shrugged. "Maybe."

"Yeah, you're definitely the glitch in the matrix. I'm convinced."

Liv took another tentative step, grateful when her foot met a firm surface.

"So what would have happened if I hadn't figured it out and actually fell?" Liv asked.

"You would have burned to death," Plato answered.

"But the lava isn't real," she argued.

"It doesn't matter if something is real or not. Things are constructed based on how we think about them. Our thoughts shape our reality. The way we perceive things makes it dangerous or harmless. To some, the sight of the ocean is peaceful, while to others, it is turbulent and scary. The ocean didn't change in either scenario, though."

"So, our thoughts are what can get us killed?" Liv asked.

"If we allow them to," Plato answered. "We always have a choice, though.

Liv was grateful when she came to the end of the rickety bridge. She realized Plato was right in front of her, standing beside the castle door.

"Hey, you didn't cross the bridge. Are you going to be able to enter the castle?" she asked him.

"Remember, there is no bridge," he said, looking behind her.

She turned to find she was standing on the edge of a cliff and had just traversed a narrow and steep path that was barely two inches wide. The rocks crumbled underfoot, falling into a deep ravine.

Liv's head jerked up. She knew at once that what she was seeing was the real landscape. The bridge had been fake, which meant what was at her back should be real.

She turned, mesmerized by the castle that stood at the top of the mountain.

CHAPTER SIXTEEN

"Do you think I should knock?" Liv asked the lynx at her side.

"You can try," Plato offered.

Liv had a hard time wrapping her mind around this strange castle. It was confounding to her that she'd stepped off the side of the mountain, walked on thin air, and arrived at a seemingly real castle at the actual top of Mount McLoughlin.

Pulling out the parchment, Liv decided to consult it. To her surprise, it was blank.

"I guess Bermuda doesn't have any words of wisdom about what to do next," Liv stated, raising her fist to knock on the broad door that towered over her. "Oh, well. I think this next part should be easy."

"I really wished you hadn't said that," Plato stated dully.

She shook her head at him.

The magic that formed the House of Fourteen was impressive, disguising it and also making it into more of a living creature than a building. But the magic at work on

Rooster's castle was just as unique. Strangely, it didn't put Liv on edge. Instead, she felt a weird sense of welcome, like the castle wanted her to enter.

Just before she rapped at the door, something threw her backward. The force was so great it made her tumble, her feet going over her head as she did a clumsy flip. Liv's legs flew over the side of the cliff, spurred by the momentum of the assault.

Her hands caught the edge. Her fingers really had to dig into the dirt to keep her hold. She didn't dare look down because she already knew she was dangling dangerously off the side of the mountain, seconds from falling to her death.

Her hands slipped, nearly making her lose it. Liv really thought she was a goner, but something clapped down hard on the back of her hands. She sucked in a breath, inhaling dirt from the rock where she was hanging.

The force that had stopped her from falling dragged her hands forward several inches, pulling her up. Grateful for the help, Liv swung her leg over the side of the cliff as she simultaneously scrambled on her elbows. She didn't stop crawling until she was several feet from the edge.

Heaving on ragged breaths, she wiped the sweat from her face.

"Is it too soon for me to remind you that you shouldn't jinx yourself?" Plato asked.

Liv gave him a seething glare. "Never is too soon."

"Well, I'm only trying to help."

Liv pushed herself to her feet, dusting off the dirt. "Thanks for saving me."

"I didn't do a thing," he lied.

"Sure, sure," she said, turning to face the door again. "I don't want that to happen again."

"Maybe you shouldn't knock," Plato suggested.

Liv nodded, striding fast for the door. When she was almost to it again, she felt the same force trying to push her back. This time, though, she sped up, barreling forward until her hand pushed the handle and she threw door back.

It swung, landing against the interior wall with a loud crack. Dust and other smells of old swept from the open castle, making Liv's nose twitch.

The entryway was dark and cavernous. In the center was a round table filled with gifts covered in dust. Now that Liv was starting to catch her breath, she realized the gothic castle was decorated as if for a party.

Three hallways led in different directions and a set of steps covered in drab red carpet ran up to the second story. However, Liv's attention brought her over to the pictures lining the stone wall.

The first was of a young man sitting regally on a grassy knoll, this exact castle behind him. It wasn't hanging precariously on the edge of a mountain in the photo. The man appeared happy, his blond hair pushed back and an easy smile on his face.

"Okay," Liv said, drawing out the word and trying to figure out the clues there.

"Do you hear that?" Plato asked.

Liv glanced around. She hadn't heard anything. Strangely, the place was incredibly quiet and still. And if Plato was there, it meant there wasn't anyone around. He always disappeared when others showed up.

"I don't," she answered.

His ears arched backward as if picking up on a noise. "Be really quiet. It's quite faint."

Liv squinted, like that would somehow help her ears work better. Still there was nothing.

She shook her head at the cat. "What is it that you hear?"

"I'm not sure," he said truthfully. "Maybe a drum?"

Liv blinked. She definitely didn't hear a drum. There was only silence.

Shrugging, she continued to study the pictures on the wall. The next was of the young man with three other guys. They had their arms around each other's shoulders and wide grins on their faces. Again, the castle was in the background.

In the next set of photos, the guy was holding a guitar or singing, and sometimes he was alone or joined by one of the other men from the second photo. They appeared to have formed a band.

As if cued by her discovery, Liv noticed that hanging on the walls were different musical artifacts. Platinum records, instruments, sheet music. Everything was so coated in dust that it was hard to make out its original color. Liv brushed her hand over one of the albums on the wall, squinting to read what was written on it.

"Moldy Oranges," she said. "That's the name of the band."

"Oh, yeah, I remember them," Plato said. "They were bigger than the Beatles."

"How is that possible? I've never heard of them."

"Well, they sort of disappeared, and all traces of them as

well. Strange things happen when magicians pursue creative endeavors. Please remember that, Liv."

"Don't worry," she answered. "I don't plan on writing so much as a limerick."

"That's good, because I've heard you trying to rhyme, and it su—"

"Hey, now!" she interrupted.

"I was going to say it supersedes your ability to clean the toilet."

She scowled at him. "I get that I'm not a great house-keeper, but you're the one who keeps trying to drink out of the toilet, which really reflects poorly on your decision-making."

"I'm a cat, what can I say?"

Liv continued to follow the photos on the wall. In the next, the guy was with a girl. She was incredibly beautiful, her long brown hair trailing down her back. Her eyes were on the camera, but the man seemed to see only her.

In the next several photographs, the girl was beside the band at ribbon-cuttings, concerts, and other special events. Liv couldn't figure out what the pictures were telling her until she got to the next one.

It was a photo of the girl holding out her hand, an enormous engagement ring on it and a satisfied smile on her face. Behind her was the castle.

Liv kept strolling, expecting to find more photos, but they ended rather rapidly. Instead, there was just a long hallway that led to a large dining room.

Liv felt like she was the first guest to arrive at a party when she stepped into the area. The table was set for at least a hundred guests with the finest china she'd ever seen. Beside the place settings were trinkets and name cards.

Carefully, Liv picked up one of the items beside the namecard and read the small card attached to it.

"We thank you for being a part of our special day. May you always find the music in your own heart, as we have found it in each other's."

Liv dropped the party favor on the table like it was coated in germs. "Oh, I get it."

"A wedding gone awry," Plato said, strolling through the dining hall. "We've all been there."

"Have we?" Liv questioned. "Wait, have *you*?"

He shook his head. "In spirit, mostly."

"So this was supposed to be Rooster's wedding," Liv said, remembering that Bermuda had mentioned he was heartbroken and tortured about something.

"I think there is still much to learn," Plato said, continuing to the room the dining hall led to. Liv hurried after him.

The next room was decorated almost as beautifully as Rudolf's coronation hall. Even though the colors of the decorations were muted due to dust and age, Liv still could tell that it had once been astonishing. It was where the wedding ceremony would have been held.

Wilted flower petals covered the runner. At the front, two candles had half-burned before being extinguished. The light that filtered through the stained glass window showed a blood-red stain covering the carpet where the bride and groom would have stood.

"Oh, no," Liv said with a gasp.

"Yes, I fear you're right."

"Right about what?" Liv asked Plato.

"Right about our groom murdering someone on his wedding day," he answered.

"I didn't say that out loud," Liv fired back, heat in her voice.

"Oh, didn't you?" Plato teased.

She growled, continuing through a door at the back. There she found a vanity set up with makeup and a veil strewn across the floor. There were also pieces of a picture that had been torn up.

With a flick of Liv's finger, the pieces rose into the air and put themselves together. When it was whole, she pulled the photo closer. It was of the girl Rooster was engaged to marry, and she was happy. Much happier than she'd been in any of the photos with him. However, beside her wasn't Rooster, but Liv did recognize the person. It was one of the band members. The drummer.

Liv dropped the picture down and stared at Plato. "Did you say you heard a drum?"

He nodded. "Or something like it."

"What if Rooster killed the drummer of his band, Moldy Oranges?" Liv wondered out loud. "Because he found out on his wedding day that his fiancée was in love with the drummer and not him?"

"That's a reasonable conclusion, based on the clues we've found," Plato said.

The room, like all the ones so far, seemed to lead to another one. She started for the door when a noise stopped her, making a chill run down her back.

It wasn't a drumbeat. She knew the difference. She'd recognize that sound anywhere. It was as old as she was. It was akin to her earliest memories. It was what anchored all mammals to the Earth.

Bu-bump.

Bu-bump.

Very clearly, Liv could hear the rhythmic beat of a heart. It was coming from nowhere and everywhere. It was faint and also loud. It was all around them, and also coming from the faint recesses of the castle.

It was Rooster's heart.

She absolutely knew it.

CHAPTER SEVENTEEN

"Do you hear that?" Liv asked Plato as they set back out into the ceremonial hall. It didn't feel right to her to continue past the bride's quarters. Something in her core told her the answers she sought were elsewhere.

He gave her an annoyed expression. "Oh, welcome to the party."

"Talk about bad timing on your part," she said, indicating the bloodstain on the floor. "I don't think anyone is partying?"

"But you hear it now?"

"Well, you're in my head. What do you think?"

"That's not how it works," he corrected.

"How am I supposed to know?" Liv asked. "Can you just hear my thoughts, or also see what I see or hear what I hear? It's all very confusing."

"Believe me, you have no idea."

Liv rolled her eyes and continued back the way she'd come.

"So where is Rooster?" Liv wondered. "And has he been

hanging out in this depressing castle all this time, reliving this horrible day?"

A shadow crossed in front of Liv, making her come to a sudden halt. She shivered but wasn't sure exactly why. At her core, she felt like there was someone else in the room, but when she turned around, the banquet hall was empty.

Deciding it was her imagination, she continued on to the dining area.

"Do you have a strange feeling that we're being watched?" Plato asked her.

"You're better at this than I am," she answered. "Do you?"

"Well, you know how I know when others are around?" he questioned.

"You disappear?"

"Just like a good friend would," he teased.

"And yes, I know what you mean."

"Well, I'm not getting that feeling right now," he stated. "I feel like we're all alone, and yet, I have the distinct impression we're not."

Liv spun around suddenly as if trying to catch someone following her. There was no one there. "Yeah, well, maybe you're losing your mind, dear Plato."

"I've been saying the same about you after your recent thoughts," he related.

"Oh, shush it," Liv said, pausing once they were back in the entryway. Again, the shadow crossed over her, like clouds going in front of the sun, but there were no large windows to make that happen. The lights in the castle were dim, so she wasn't sure where the shadow would be coming from.

She studied the photos once more, not finding anything new, then turned to Plato.

"What do you suppose we do now?" she asked him.

The constant beating in the background was hard to ignore, but it was also sort of soothing.

"Why don't you see if Bermuda offered anything new about this case?" he suggested.

She consented, slipping her hand into her pocket to retrieve the piece of parchment. As soon as she pulled it from her cape, words scrolled across it.

"To find Rooster, you must first locate his heart. Reunite him with it, and he might help you. Otherwise, finding the Mortal Seven will be impossible."

CHAPTER EIGHTEEN

"So no pressure, right?" Liv joked, putting the parchment away. "I just have to find an organ somewhere in this massive castle.

"He must have removed his heart because he couldn't bear the pain," Plato said slowly, putting it all together.

"You can do that?" Liv asked.

"Well, it's isn't safe, as you can imagine. However, with magic, you can do just about anything," Plato explained. "And as you can see from the castle, Rooster is a very skilled magician."

Looking up the stairs, Liv tried to hone in on where the sound of the heart was coming from. At times, it was louder than others. Sometimes it seemed to be coming from above her, and other times from behind her. She thought it was safe to assume that this wouldn't be straightforward or easy.

"What if he doesn't want his heart back?" Liv asked as she began to climb the stairs. "He did take it out for a reason, after all."

"That's a good point," Plato said, following her. "However, once you remove a heart, it isn't easy to reconnect with it. He might not be able to put it back in. Also, the reason he wanted to separate himself from his heart might not be worth the pain of not having it. Strangely, our hearts are what let us feel emotions, but without them, we suffer greatly. I suspect Rooster is tortured without his heart."

The dark shadow swept overhead again, momentarily casting them in darkness. Liv spun and pulled Bellator from her sheath. She stood frozen for several seconds, waiting to see if there would be more mysterious movement. When nothing happened, she climbed to the top of the stairs.

As she suspected, the castle was vast, the seemingly unending hallway going on farther in both directions than she could properly see. It was lined with doors. Beside many of the doors were suits of metal armor with large swords, arranged to look like soldiers guarding.

"It's going to take a while to search all these rooms," Liv stated. "We could split up."

Plato shook his head. "I don't think blindly searching the rooms is a good idea."

Liv tried the first door, finding it locked. "Well, and since I'm guessing most of the rooms will be locked, that's definitely not going to work."

"We just have to think like a broken-hearted man," Plato suggested. "You've just found out on your wedding day that your bride is in love with your friend. You lash out, killing him—"

"Or maybe her," Liv interrupted.

"That's right," Plato corrected. "Yes, he could have killed the girl."

"So then you lock yourself inside this castle and remove your heart," Liv mused.

Bu-bump. Bu-bump.

The echo of Rooster's beating heart seemed to mock Liv as she tried to figure out this mystery.

"Wait, what did the inscription on the party favor say?" Liv asked.

"We thank you for being a part of our special day," Plato answered.

She shook her head at him. "No, the other part."

"Oh, I believe it said, 'May you always find the music in your own heart, as we have found it in each other's.'"

"So what if he locked it away with his music?" Liv offered. "Music would make him feel. Without it, he would be free of his heartache."

Plato nodded. "Yes, that makes sense. It would be how he could have worked such a powerful spell."

"How do you figure?" Liv asked.

"Well, one would need a method for removing the heart," Plato began. "Notes from a sad ballad might work. But once the heart was out of his chest, he'd have to keep it somewhere safe. The heart works in very symbolic ways."

"So, his guitar?" Liv posed. "Do you think that's where he keeps his heart?"

"It's possible," Plato said, searching the long hallway. "Now the question is, where does he keep his guitar?"

Liv drew a breath and muttered an incantation her mother had taught her early on. It was a locating spell that only worked when an object was of major importance and was hard to find.

From her back, she heard a muffled banging. Liv whipped around, running in the direction of the noise, passing a dozen doors and as many suits of armor. She slowed when the banging grew louder.

Ahead a door shook every time the banging sounded.

"Do you think?" Liv asked Plato.

"That the guitar you just located is trying to get out of the door? Yes, I'd say so."

"Well, this was easy," she said, striding forward. Then she halted. Looked down at Plato. "I just jinxed myself, didn't I?"

He nodded, a heavy look on his face. "I'm afraid so."

CHAPTER NINETEEN

In unison, the metal suits of armor all came alive in the hallway. Like soldiers, they snapped to attention, facing Liv.

In front of her were six phantom soldiers carrying long swords. Behind her were another six.

"Oh, hell," Liv muttered, readying Bellator. "You try to help a guy out by reuniting him with his heart, and this is how he repays you?"

"Remember, part of him is afraid to feel again," Plato said.

"Good point," Liv said, whipping her head back and forth, trying to keep an eye on the enemies approaching from both directions. "There are a lot of these guys. Any ideas?"

"Duck," Plato yelled.

Liv spun just as one of the suits of armor leapt through the air, swinging its sword at her. She dropped to the ground, kicking her leg around and taking out its legs from under it.

Immediately she jumped up, grabbing her shin. "Damn it! That hurt!"

"They are covered in metal," Plato said, casually sitting to the side and licking his paw.

"Thanks," Liv said without any gratitude in her tone. "Care to change into a lion and help me defeat these guys?"

The closest one was only five feet away, moving like a clumsy robot.

"I would, but I can't," Plato said.

Liv produced a fireball and launched it at the clunky soldier nearing her.

"Because?" she asked as the fireball ricocheted off the chest plate and sped back in her direction. She had to drop to the floor to avoid being hit by her own attack. The fireball blasted into a soldier on her other side, knocking it back into more, making them fall like dominos.

"Because it's bath time," Plato answered simply.

The screeching of metal as the soldiers tried to untangle their limbs from each other made Liv squint.

"Well, maybe when you're done licking your butt," she said, throwing a blast of wind at the suit of armor on her other side. The domino effect had given her an idea.

"After my bath, it is time for my early-afternoon nap," Plato stated.

The blast of wind sent the five approaching suits to the ground in a cacophony of noise. "What about after that?" Liv asked, spinning around to the side. Unfortunately, the suits had recovered, rising back into formation.

"After my early-afternoon nap, I have a small gap of free time before my mid-afternoon nap," Plato said. "But I'm pretty busy after that."

Liv rolled her eyes. "Because then you have your late-afternoon nap, which is right before your early-evening nap."

"You do pay attention," Plato said, licking his hindquarters.

The soldiers were too close for her to try another elemental spell on them, and that had only knocked them down. What she needed to do was disable them, which meant only one thing would work. She brought Bellator up and around, smashing into the helmet of the closest suit. It shot off, flying toward where Plato was casually bathing. Just before hitting him, it redirected, shooting like a cannonball at the suits on the other side of them. The attack made one soldier explode into loose bits of metals.

Liv ducked to avoid the shrapnel. "See, you helped."

"No, that was just luck," he lied.

One of the suits grabbed Liv, clamping its strong arms around her and making her drop Bellator. She kicked, wiggling furiously to get her arms unlocked from its grip. "Want to throw some more luck at me, Plato?" Liv asked breathlessly as the robotic armor grabbed at from her either side. She went from having an advantage to being nearly surrounded.

The lynx stretched before settling down into a resting position. "I would, but I skipped my late-morning nap, so I'm pretty exhausted."

Even with the turmoil of being seconds from being ripped apart, something suddenly occurred to Liv.

"That's a great idea," she said between measured breaths.

"Thanks. Napping is always a good idea," Plato said, his

voice trailing off as he slept while chaos continued to reign in front of him.

Liv lifted her legs up, making the suit holding her nearly topple backward. That made the other soldiers lose their grip on her momentarily. She used this tiny window to mutter a strong incantation, one she knew would drain most of her reserves. For a moment, she wasn't sure if it had worked.

And then one by one, the suits of armor began to slump to the floor like it was suddenly their nap time too. The ones grabbing for her lost interest, slouching against the wall and sliding down, their helmets resting to the side. However, the one that was holding her didn't let go.

She didn't understand. She'd used her reserves to cast a strong sleeping spell on the soldiers. It worked because they were supposed to behave the same as whole individuals, and therefore, magical law dictated that spells affected them the same way as an actual person. However, if this one soldier wasn't falling asleep like the piles of metal lying on the floor, it meant only one thing.

The soldier holding her wasn't a whole person.

It was Rooster.

CHAPTER TWENTY

Liv struggled, trying to free her pinned hands. However, Rooster was strong, holding her arms against her body as he carried her backward.

She yelled and kicked her legs, but that did her no good. Her energy was extremely depleted from the sleeping spell, and Plato appeared to be completely passed out.

"Damn it! Rooster! I'm trying to help you. I'm Liv Beaufont. I'm a Warrior for the House of Fourteen!" Liv yelled, squirming the best she could.

He was carrying her through the hallway, moving fast as if she weighed little. Liv ran through possible spells in her head that she could cast to incapacitate the magician, but all the ones she thought could work would take more energy than she had.

The armor slammed through a door, making it swing back violently, knocking into Liv. She continued to kick and squirm, not budging from his tight grasp.

The room they'd entered was darker than the hallway, and even over her struggling against the suit of armor, she could hear strange music filling the space. It was eerie, and brought strange images of darkness and death to her mind.

Thinking the music signaled her end, Liv prepared to use a spell that would most assuredly rob her of all of her energy. If it worked, she'd be free, but it would demolish the magician holding her. There was the very real possibility it would also end her.

She pressed her eyes shut and started the complicated arrangement of words. Liv felt the energy flow out of her and had to force herself to continue. However, when she was dropped to the hard floor, her words stopped, and her eyes popped open.

Springing to her feet, Liv prepared to fight. To finish the complicated spell. To do whatever it took to defeat the deranged magician. However, the suit of armor had backed up to the wall after depositing her on the floor. Rooster had his arm extended and was pointing at a man lying in the middle of the dim room.

At first, Liv thought it was the drummer he'd killed. She gasped as the realization came over her. A small beam of light from the only window in the room illuminated the body, showing her the one thing she'd been missing.

Lying on the surface of a table was Rooster, his blond hair brushed back and a grief-stricken expression on his young face. His eyes were closed and he was wearing a tuxedo, but in the center of his chest was a large bloodstain, the fabric ripped.

Liv glanced between the motionless form on the table and the suit of armor as it all came together. "You didn't kill them. You ripped your own heart out in front of everyone."

The screech of metal made Liv flinch when he nodded.

"And your friend? Your bride?" Liv asked, thinking she already knew the answer. "They ran away together, didn't they?"

Another nod.

Liv's own heart began to ache for the man or the fraction of the man before her. He'd done something most wouldn't have been able to survive, and yet here he was.

"But you don't have to live with the torment anymore," Liv said, trying to figure out what she was missing. Rooster wanted her help. She could feel it. And yet, he was afraid. That was the reason he'd knocked her back from the front door and sent soldiers after her. But he'd brought her here to the room with his body, and there was an important reason for that, she realized.

Liv closed her eyes, listening intently to the music that filled the room. It seemed to get louder with her eyes shut. Suddenly she realized that the music had lyrics. They were so faint at first she could hardly understand them. But then it hit her, nearly making her double over from the realization.

"May you always find the music in your own heart, as we have found it in each other's," a soulful voice sang, weaving together the full story for Liv.

Her eyes sprang open. "You're afraid she stole your voice, aren't you? You believe she was the inspiration behind your creativity, and without her, you're forever lost?"

The metal screeching told Liv the armor was nodding even before she could see it.

"But Moldy Oranges was big before her," Liv stated.

"And all your music has disappeared from the Earth; not because she's gone, but because you disappeared. Rooster, you don't need her to find the music in your heart. You never did. It's always been inside you."

They were only words. Silly words of compassion that many could dismiss as trivial. Unimportant. Inconsequential. This man, this musician, had lived for so long in this castle. How could Liv expect to change him by stating what she felt was the obvious truth? And then she realized that that was how battles of the heart were won. Love confounds most, but when someone with an objective perspective points out the truth, it has the power to shatter the illusions that chain the heartbroken to the Earth.

As if suddenly unchained, the suit of armor bolted forward.

Liv, fearing he'd gone crazy again, backed away rapidly, finding the opposite wall. However, her fear quickly dissipated when he simply removed something from the hand of the body.

Curiously, Liv leaned forward as he offered it to her. A shiny key winked through the darkness of the room.

"You want your heart back?" she asked, realizing she could not give it back to him without his consent.

He nodded, the screeching of his helmet strangely accompanying the music.

Liv took the key and sprinted out the open door and down the hallway.

Bu-bump.

Bu-bump.

The beating of Rooster's heart was like thunder during

a storm. Liv could feel it shaking the castle. It rattled the floor and made her nearly bang into the wall.

She skidded to a halt next to the door where Plato soundlessly slept. With shaking fingers, she slipped the key into the lock, pushing the door open.

It was another dark, nondescript room. However, lying on the mostly empty floor was an electric guitar.

Just like in the center of Rooster's chest, there was a hole in the front of the instrument.

Carefully, Liv picked up the guitar and quickly carried it back the way she'd come.

Bu-bump.

Bu-bump.

The beating of the heart was so loud it was almost deafening, but Liv continued walking, focused on her mission.

When she entered the room, the suit of armor straightened suddenly, adding a screeching sound to the mix of beating heart and the sad ballad playing on repeat.

Trying to hide the grimace on her face, she reached into the guitar until she felt the wet, squishy organ deep inside the recess of the instrument. As carefully as she could, she pulled it free, watching as Rooster's heart beat in her hands.

Bu-bump.

Bu-bump.

Liv was fascinated that a human's heart could beat outside the body. It proved to her the power of love. That in itself was our lifeforce. Breathing was only secondary to loving.

Fueled by a strange instinct, Liv plunged the heart into

the opening in Rooster's chest. She stood back, not knowing what else to do.

Nothing happened.

She worried she'd done something wrong. Messed it up. Killed Rooster for good.

But then the suit of armor spilled to the ground with a loud clanking noise. A dark shadow rose from the metal, and she caught the faint outline of a man. He zoomed by her like Peter Pan flying through the air. As if magnetized, the shadow slipped into the resting body.

At once, Rooster shot into a sitting position, choking and coughing, clutching his chest. The music in the room, the beating of the heart, and the darkness disappeared, replaced by light.

Liv glanced around to notice they were in a beautifully decorated office. Rooster blinked, seemingly disoriented as he slipped his legs over the side of his desk, staring around and trying to regain his focus.

His attention finally landed on Liv. He was to his feet at once, nearly falling to his knees. Liv caught him with an outstretched hand, holding him upright.

"Are you okay?" she asked the magician before her.

Even though his tuxedo was covered with dust and blood, he nodded and smiled, a new light in his eyes. "Yes, and you, Liv Beaufont, are a musician's friend."

CHAPTER TWENTY-ONE

Liv took Rooster's arm when he presented it to her, offering to accompany her out of the castle.

"I have much to do," he said, glancing around the dusty hallway as they strode for the stairs.

The castle that had been full of darkness and shadows was now suddenly filled with color. Liv was amazed at how beautiful the paintings that lined the walls were. She hadn't noticed them before. She peered up at the intricate pattern on the ceiling. The ancient castle was like something out of a museum.

When they were almost to the stairs, Liv pulled away from Rooster. "I'm sorry. I almost forgot something."

She sped down to where the suits of armor were resting. They were all back into their respective places as if a battle hadn't happened there. She plucked Bellator from the floor, sheathing it.

When she returned to where Rooster was patiently waiting for her, he said, "What about your cat? Will he be okay there?"

Liv cast a glance over her shoulder. Plato was seemingly asleep. "Yes. He has tuckered himself out not helping me."

She took the arm he held out for her and started down the long staircase to the main entryway. To her amazement, the gifts from the wedding were gone. So were the pictures that had been lining the wall. A quick peek toward the back told her the wedding decorations had disappeared as well.

When she turned back to Rooster, he was wearing a calm expression. "I figured it was time to redecorate. What do you think?"

She nodded proudly, amazed by how fast he'd changed everything. He was one powerful magician. "Yes, that seems like a good idea. Will you stay here?"

He glanced around. "Oh, yes. This is my home. It always has been. But I think I'll be relocating it. Getting to the grocery store is quite the pain from this location."

Liv laughed. "I hope you don't mind, but I did seek you out for a reason."

Rooster tilted his head to the side. "Was it to steal my heart? Because you might have succeeded at that." He winked at her, and Liv was very aware of this man's charm. Give him a guitar and a microphone, and every woman on Earth would be dying to be his. Not Liv, though.

She smiled. "My heart actually belongs to another."

"Oh, what a lucky man," he said with a genuine grin.

"Although we can't be together," she said, surprised she was confiding this to a stranger.

He tilted his head. "That's how the best stories begin. True love will always prevail, though."

Her insides were suddenly rattling around with nervousness. There was that word again: love.

Maybe sensing her anxiety, Rooster gave her an easy smile. "And what is your request?"

"I need to know how to make a chimera reveal itself," she stated.

He nodded, his eyes growing distant. "That's a beautiful spell. One I haven't thought about in quite some time. But first let me ask you, do you know of a chimera? They are rare."

"I know there are at least seven out there that I have to find," Liv answered.

"How is your singing voice?" he asked her.

She pursed her lips. "I'm afraid that's not my specialty."

He nodded, a knowing look on his face. "But that's all subject to change."

Rooster lifted his palm into the air and blew. Although Liv hadn't seen anything in his hand, sparkling dust spread over her face, covering her in a cool mist. Suddenly she had music buzzing in her head.

It made her instantly start humming. Rooster smiled widely, looking like the young man she'd seen in the photos lining the walls. "And now you know the song of the chimera. Sing it for them, and they will reveal themselves."

Feeling suddenly light, with a strange buzzing in her head, Liv strode to the entrance of the castle. She was absolutely stunned to find they weren't located on the top of Mount McLoughlin in Southern Oregon. The castle had relocated to a grassy meadow with rolling hills and streams in the distance.

She spun to face Rooster, her mouth open. "You already… But how?"

His eyes sparkled with delight. "I simply moved back to where I belong."

She shook her head at the incredible magician before her. "You are something else, Rooster. What's next for you?"

He mused, staring at the blue skies and white puffy clouds rolling toward the castle, which was no longer covered in snow. "I think it's time I get the old band together—minus one member, though. Do you happen to know any drummers?"

Liv laughed. "I don't. But I'd love to go to one of your concerts when you tour."

He nodded, lifting her hand to his lips and kissing it. "I think you should be in the front row. I can guarantee there will be a new song or two dedicated to you, Warrior Beaufont. Good luck with your adventures."

CHAPTER TWENTY-TWO

"Are you insane?" Clark asked Liv, tapping the large leather-bound book she'd given him.

The Black Void loomed in the distance, but she tried to ignore that it was even more colorful than before. She'd pointed it out to her brother, but like everyone else, he couldn't see it.

"Yes, of course, I'm insane, which is why the council gets to send me off on ridiculous missions where I risk my life." She flashed him a pleading smile. "But please, I need your help."

He held up the book she'd shoved into his arms moments prior. "You didn't have to give me this book. I already knew the law. Everyone knows the law, even if these books have long been buried."

Adler had apparently made many books go missing that detailed the House of Fourteen's laws and history. That was better for him, so that no one learned any clues about mortals once being a part of the House.

"I didn't know the law," she confessed. "And neither did

Stefan."

Clark shook his head. "Then you're fine. Just end things, and you won't have to worry about getting in trouble. If it ever comes up, you can simply plead innocence, and the missing history books will support your case."

Adamantly, Liv shook her head. "We don't want to end things and move on. We want to change the law."

"No, Liv, that's not how it works. You can't simply change what the Founders stated as laws when they created the House of Fourteen."

"Why not?" she challenged.

He blew out an exasperated breath. "Because it's…well, it…I don't know. They are laws for a reason."

"Just because things are laws, it doesn't make them right."

He threw his free hand into the air. "How many times are you going to lecture me on laws and justice?"

"How many times are you going to fail to see that they aren't the same thing?" she fired back.

"Liv, even if there was some way to change things, I wouldn't know the first thing about how to do it. Not to mention that I'm overwhelmed by studying the *Forgotten Archives*. There's so much we don't know. And mortals are seeing magic for the first time. Well, those who aren't asleep are seeing magic. There's some strange virus going around that's causing a sleeping disorder."

"Don't worry, I'm on that case," Liv stated with confidence. "I'll have mortals awake and healthy again soon."

"Wait, you know why so many of them are sleeping most of the time?"

"Yeah, but it's a case with Father Time, and I'm not

allowed to discuss it." Her eyes darted to the Black Void, sensing she should not say much more, but not sure why.

Clark pressed his fist to his forehead. "I don't know what you want me to do here. Families can't date. And two Warriors? Well, that's absolutely cut and dried. There's too much conflict of interest."

"Stefan and I have worked tons of cases together," Liv argued. "It's because of our bond to each other that we've been successful when we should have died."

"Does this have something to do with his unprecedented success at slaughtering demons?" Clark asked.

Liv couldn't help but smile. "I'm not at liberty to discuss the secrets behind that."

Clark growled.

"Look, how many times do I ask for your help?" Liv argued.

"Well, there was when you were bitten by the lophos, and then when Queen Visa nearly killed you, and when you needed to hide Sophia's egg."

Liv laughed. "Okay, good point. But seriously, I know there's a way for us to change the law. I can't give up on this one. We're not going to risk our positions, I promise you that. We know better. But if there is any way in the world I can be with that guy? Well, I never thought I'd want that, but I do. Clark, this is not a fleeting feeling."

He gave her a look that shook her to the core. "Don't you think I know that? You haven't so much as had a crush. If you feel this way about someone, he's someone special. But I just don't know."

"Will you please just try?" Liv asked. "That's all I'm asking."

He considered her for a long moment. "Yes, of course, I will. I'll do whatever I can. But please don't get your hopes up."

Overcome by a strange joy she'd never experienced, Liv bounded forward and planted a kiss on her brother's cheek. "Thank you! You're the best."

Before she could take in his astonished face or deal with her strange show of affection, Liv sprinted through the Door of Reflection into the Chamber of the Tree.

"Mr. Ludwig," Lorenzo Rosario said as soon as Liv stumbled through the Door. "We are ready to hear your update on the elf negotiations."

"Actually, we aren't," Raina said, pointing to Clark, who came through the door behind Liv. "It is customary for us to wait until all council members are present."

"I'm sorry I'm late," Clark said, hurrying to his seat as Liv took her spot between Stefan and Spencer.

"Brushing up on House history, I see," Kayla Sinclair said, pointing to the leather-bound book in his hands.

"U-u-uhhh…" he stuttered. "Yes. Many of these volumes disappeared while Adler and Decar were in the House."

"If this is going to be another session where the Royals degrade my relatives, I'll have to object," Kayla said, her long black hair on one side falling over one of her eyes.

Liv knew there was something off about the girl, but she couldn't tell what. She glanced at Spencer beside her. He didn't appear to share any of the traits of the other

Sinclairs, but she wasn't sure that mattered. Something wasn't right about the two.

"Councilor Sinclair," Hester began. "I don't think we have to remind you that your relatives, if alive, would be liable for treason, murder, and a list of many other crimes. These are not men who hold the respect of the Royals."

Thankfully this shut the girl up.

"Well, since everyone is here," Lorenzo began, "I was hoping to get a report from Mr. Ludwig on the elf negotiations."

"They could be going better," Stefan said, standing with his feet hip's width apart and his arms behind his back.

"But?" Haro asked.

Stefan's eyes darted from side to side. "Well, I can't help but think that Warrior Sinclair is sabotaging my efforts."

There was a collective murmur around the room.

"That is a bold accusation," Lorenzo stated. "Do you have evidence to back this up?"

Liv peered sideways at Spencer, studying his face and spiky black mohawk. To her surprise, he strangely appeared unaffected by this claim. He simply stared straight ahead stoically, reminding her of the suits of armor in Rooster's castle.

"I don't," Stefan answered. "But when I've tried to track down one of the last enemies of the elves, I've been sabotaged at every turn. My weapons were destroyed at one point. After I had them replaced, the villain I was after was told of my stalking and fled before I could capture him. It's been a series of problems that I've never encountered in the past."

"Is it possible that you are the problem and not Warrior

Sinclair?" Lorenzo asked.

Liv could tell that Stefan was trying to keep his anger at bay, but it wasn't easy. "With all due respect, I don't make mistakes like those."

"I agree," Hester stated. "Warrior Ludwig has a fantastic track record. If he thinks having Warrior Sinclair shadow him is holding him back, I think we should honor that request."

"I must object," Lorenzo said, his voice suddenly loud. "How is a new Warrior supposed to learn the ropes unless they have help?"

"Warrior Beaufont managed," Raina stated.

"Yes, but…" Lorenzo's voice trailed off.

"Maybe Spencer should shadow Liv, then," Kayla offered.

"Although I would love the chance to learn more about this supposed human," Liv said, waving a hand in front of the face of the warrior beside her, "I can't help. I've got a case for Father Time."

"Yes, and that's exactly why I think that Spencer could benefit from the experience," Kayla imposed.

"We are very grateful that Father Time has chosen one of our warriors as his delegates," Raina interjected. "And we won't risk that by losing his trust. If Warrior Beaufont doesn't want to be shadowed, the discussion is closed."

"I don't think that's how democracy works," Kayla fired back.

"Then we take a vote on the matter," Haro suggested.

"He should shadow me," Trudy stated from the far end. She was usually so quiet that Liv forgot she was on the other side of Stefan.

All of the Councilors looked at her.

"I'm an experienced Warrior. Actually, I've been doing this for far longer than Warrior Beaufont." She glanced at Liv. "No offense."

"None taken," Liv retorted.

"I'd be happy to have Spencer shadow me," Trudy continued.

"Well, this seems like a good solution," Hester said with a proud smile and a discreet wink at her sister. Liv had recently learned that Trudy was keeping the secret that she was a seer. That wasn't a gift that was always revered in the magician culture. Some who wanted the future veiled got rid of seers. They had been mysteriously murdered for ages, so it wasn't a surprise to Liv that the sisters were keeping this information from everyone. However, it made Liv wonder what Trudy had seen that made her want to help her by taking on the responsibility of the newbie Sinclair.

"Well, then we'll need a proper update from you, Ms. DeVries," Lorenzo said.

In a perfectly professional and rehearsed manner, Trudy began to give her report.

Stefan cut his eyes at Liv. "I noticed that Clark has one of the law books."

She nodded minutely. "He might be able to help."

"Raina has agreed to help too," Stefan said in a whisper, a small smile hiding at the edges of his eyes.

"Don't you dare look at me like that, Warrior Ludwig."

He crossed his eyes and stuck out his tongue. "Is this better?"

Liv couldn't stop the laugh that spilled from her mouth.

"Excuse me," Lorenzo interjected, making her tense. "Is there something you want to share with the council, Ms. Beaufont?"

Her phone buzzed right on cue, as if someone knew she needed to be rescued. She pulled it from her pocket. It was a text from Mortimer.

I have the location for Zeno Dutillet, but the brownie can only give it to you in person. You have been out of mortal territory, or I would have avoided this message altogether.

Liv nodded. She had been in magical territory for the most part.

"I apologize," Liv said, recovering. "This is Father Time business. I'll have to be off."

"And this business?" Lorenzo began.

"I believe we've been told not to pry," Hester interjected.

"I think that if we at least knew that Ms. Beaufont wasn't off gallivanting, it would be better," Kayla stated.

Liv's temper flared. "I never gallivant. I haven't even taken a day off. For your information, I'm going to go relieve the problem that's putting mortals to sleep."

She turned and stormed from the chamber.

If Liv had been looking then, she would have seen the satisfied expression that sprang to Kayla's Sinclair's face. The warrior had fallen for the trick, defending herself against Kayla's accusations by spilling some of the truth.

CHAPTER TWENTY-THREE

Liv couldn't think of a more mortal place than John's electronic repair shop.

Well, except that it had had magical renovations to make it bigger, brighter, and newer. But it also had John, and he was the best mortal she knew.

He gave her a welcoming smile when she strode through the door. Pickles barked with excitement, running up to her and jumping around her heels. All she wanted to do was sing the song of the chimera to determine if she was right and Pickles was not really a dog, meaning that John was one of the Mortal Seven.

She was just about to do that when John stepped aside, revealing the tiny brownie beside him. Liv recognized him as the one who had helped her in the Natural History Museum.

"I'm guessing you can explain why this guy is hanging around here," John said with a laugh.

Liv nodded, a bit disappointed that she couldn't sing

the song to Pickles and learn the truth. "Yes. I believe he has a message for me."

Kneeling down, Liv smiled at the brownie. "You do, don't you, Freddie?"

He clapped his hands. "You remembered me! And yes, Warrior Beaufont. Mortimer has sent me to give you the location of Zeno Dutillet. However, I must warn you that he resides in a dangerous place even brownies won't venture into."

Liv let out a breath. "I sort of figured that."

"You'll need to be really careful since there are many man-eating monsters," Freddie continued.

"Yes, that seems about right."

"And Zeno Dutillet is heavily guarded," Freddie stated.

"But if I don't get to him…"

"Then mortals will sleep forever," Freddie finished her sentence.

"Why doesn't it affect me?" John stated. "I could use a nap, actually."

"I'm guessing it has something to do with your Mortal Seven blood," Liv stated.

"Oh, well, that makes sense. So you're off on another adventure?" John asked.

Liv glanced at Freddie. He handed her a piece of parchment, which she hoped wasn't as convoluted as the instructions that Bermuda had given her. "Yes, unfortunately, I'm off again. But I want to make some time to talk to you as soon as I get back."

John's face went slack. "If this is about Alicia, I can explain."

Liv's eyes drifted from side to side. "It wasn't, but I'm intrigued."

"Oh, well, I was just kidding about Alicia," he said with a fake laugh.

"No, you weren't," Liv said. "But we can discuss that later, or not at all. Your business is yours."

He laughed and waved as she started for the door. "Be careful, Liv."

"Thanks," she said, waving back. "And thanks, Freddie! You're the best!"

The brownie beamed at the compliment, his complexion growing pink. He also waved as Liv left the electronic repair shop.

CHAPTER TWENTY-FOUR

Twelve mosquito bites.

Liv had been in the swamp in Louisiana for less than an hour, and she already had a dozen bites from the little bloodsuckers. She had spells that could make her see in the dark, become invisible, change appearance, and knock down a legion of soldiers. However, she couldn't figure out the incantation to keep mosquitos off her.

Freddie's note had stated that Zeno Dutillet was hiding out somewhere in the bayous in the south of Louisiana. There were hundreds of miles of inlets and outlets of swamp passageways where he could be. The brownie apparently couldn't be more specific because, as he put it, "He's moving around a lot."

That was fine, Liv thought. She'd just have to put on her detective hat and narrow down her options. She did have magic, after all, and even if it didn't work on mosquitos, hopefully, it would help her find an ancient man who could put mortals to sleep if he wasn't asleep himself.

The idea that the SandMan had not randomly awoken

wasn't lost on Liv. It had been strange timing. They'd finally gotten rid of Adler and Decar, awoken mortals to magic, and freed the lost history, and then, bam, the SandMan comes back from a century of slumber. And what does he do? Put mortals to sleep. The whole thing reeked, but she needed more information before drawing conclusions.

She slapped her arm. "And bug repellant. I need freaking bug repellant. And a boat."

Liv crossed the parking lot of Jeb's Trading Post, scowling at the graffitied chair out front. The brownie had given her a location down by the docks, half a mile away. After walking up and down the rocky bank, she'd decided it was time to enlist some help.

The door chimed when she strolled into the small shop, which smelled like fish and rot. A man in overalls with a blank expression looked up from his crossword when she entered.

"Are you Jeb?" she asked, flashing a forced smile.

"The one and only," he said, his Southern drawl sort of endearing.

"I need a boat, Jeb," she stated. "It says out front you rent them."

"They are all being used," he said at once.

"But I saw a whole line of them at the side of your shop," she argued.

"Those need to be repaired."

"Well, I'm actually in the repair business," Liv countered. "Maybe I can fix them in return for using one."

"I don't think so," the man said, scowling at her without reason.

"Okay, it sounds like you're not in the business of making money." Liv picked up a bottle of bug spray. "Will you object if I pay you real cash for this?"

He lifted an eyebrow, seeming to consider the proposition. "I don't see why. It's six dollars, and I need exact change."

Liv returned the skeptical expression. "Yeah, that's not a problem, Jeb."

She strode over and laid down the money. "Do you know of another place that rents boats?"

"I'm afraid not," he said, no remorse in his mechanical tone.

"Hmmmm. That's strange. There are miles and miles of swamps, and strangely no boats for hire."

"It's our busy time of year," he stated.

"Yes, and it seems I'm in the wrong line of business," Liv said. "Guess I need to set up shop next to you."

If Jeb was offended by that, he didn't show it.

"How about a bathroom?" Liv asked, pointing to a door at the back. "I've been on the road for a while, and could use a break."

He stood to the side, making a wall between her and the counter, protective menace in his eyes. "There's no public restrooms here. You're best moving on."

Liv took a step backward, unnerved by the strange blankness in his eyes. She'd seen that expression before recently, but couldn't place it.

"Okay, sorry for troubling you," Liv stated. "I'll be on my way."

Without another word, Liv strode out of Jeb's Trading Post, the strangest feeling tickling her spine with unease.

Kayla Sinclair waited until the door was completely shut and Olivia Beaufont had marched across the dusty parking lot.

She closed her hand, making the illusion of Jeb disappear. When she'd been in the Chamber of the Tree, she'd suspected that Olivia had found the location of the Sand-Man. Just as Talon had stated, this girl didn't quit. That was fine. If this Beaufont wanted to hunt around in the swamps for Zeno Dutillet, she was going to regret it.

Kayla Sinclair flexed her hands by her sides, ready to do whatever it took to stop this warrior from putting the SandMan to sleep.

CHAPTER TWENTY-FIVE

The boats at the side of Jeb's store looked fine, but Liv wasn't going to argue with the local. Instead, she spotted a truck with a boat getting gas at the pump. Pulling down her hood and fanning out her hair, she summoned her best Southern charm.

She sidled up to the side of the truck, plastering a smile on her face. It dropped as soon as she peered into the compartment. The guy behind the wheel, a young man with a beard that made him appear much older than he was, slept with his head back and his mouth wide open.

The SandMan had struck again. At least the guy wasn't driving. Liv peered over the side of the bed and noticed that the pump was done filling the tank. Who knew how long this guy had been there sleeping in his car while getting gas?

Liv leaned back to the window. "Hey, Mister. Wake up."

The guy didn't budge.

She snapped, making a sharp clicking sound.

Still nothing.

She thought about dowsing him in water, but when he came to, he might not be happy with her, and she needed his help.

Liv remembered the sleeping spell she'd put on the suits of armor. What the SandMan could do was obviously much more intense than her spell, but it gave her an idea. Reversing spells wasn't easy and sometimes had strange results, but she thought in this instance, she could chance it, even without knowing the proper incantation. Liv recited the words under her breath, carefully trying to do the spell exactly as she'd done it before, but in reverse. When it was done, she straightened, holding her breath and hoping for the best.

"If it works, then—"

The guy bolted upright, jumping so high he hit his head on the roof of his truck. Grabbing his head, he looked around, disoriented. "What? Where am I? What's going on?"

Liv smiled, batting her eyelashes at him. "You appeared to have fallen asleep. It must be this humidity."

He blinked at her in confusion. "And who are you?"

"I'm Liv," she said, extending a hand to him.

He took it, shaking it with more fervor than she thought necessary. "I'm Al. And wow, I feel awake. I can't remember when I've felt this alert."

And there was the side effect, Liv thought with minor regret. The spell would wear off in a day or two. Until then, this guy would be wide-eyed and probably more productive than he'd ever been.

"Well, Al, I'm looking to rent a boat."

He pointed at Jeb's Trading Post. "You can do that there. They've got a lot of swell options."

Liv glanced over her shoulder at the store. "Yeah, apparently they can't help me."

Al's brow scrunched in confusion. "Really? That's weird."

"That was my thought too, but maybe you can help me out. How much to rent your boat here?" Liv pointed to the flat-bottom aluminum boat on the trailer behind the truck. It sat twelve people and appeared to be patched in several places.

"Oh, I don't rent my boat out," he said, shaking his head. "I give swamp tours. Can I interest you in one of those, Miss?"

Liv feigned a polite smile. "No, thank you. I really need to get out on the water on my own."

Al scratched his head. "With all due respect, ma'am, I reckon you're not from around here."

Liv glanced down at her all-black clothing and the cape that hid Bellator on her hip. *What gave it away?* she thought.

"Is that a problem?" she asked.

He shook his head. "Not at all. I make my living from tourism. But it's just that if you aren't acquainted with the swamp, well, you can get mighty lost out there. Why do you want to take a boat out on your own, anyway?"

This guy was genuinely nice. Liv could see it in his eyes. For that reason, and many others, she didn't want to use any brainwashing on him. She only did that when absolutely necessary.

"I'm looking for someone, actually," Liv said discreetly.

"In the swamp?" Al asked. "Like a missing person? Have you called the authorities?"

"No, it's more like a guy who I suspect doesn't want to be found. A criminal of sorts."

The guy's face contorted with surprise. "Again, have you contacted the authorities?"

"It's not really one of those criminals the police can track down," Liv explained.

"Oh, you're like one of those private detective types, aren't you?" he asked with awe.

"Something like that."

Al pulled his hat off his head and ruffled his dark-brown hair, making it spike from the sweat. "Well, between you and me, there are some questionable things going on in the swamp right now. I've been giving tours for over seven years, and recently, I've seen things no one can explain or comprehend."

"Like what?" Liv asked.

The guy stuck his hat back on his head and showed her a sheepish expression. "You'll think I'm crazy if I say it."

"Try me," Liv encouraged.

"Well, I know it sounds nuts, but some of the stuff is like magic. The animals, well, they don't act normal anymore. Some of them don't look normal, either. And, well, it's hard to explain all the strangeness going on out there."

Liv nodded. "Yes, I've heard about these strange events."

"Is that why you're going out to the swamp?" Al asked. "Are you investigating these weird happenings? Is your criminal behind them?"

Liv thought about that for a moment. This mortal was

seeing magic for the first time ever. That would be a lot to process. Maybe she could help him understand it, but she'd need to ease him into the new reality.

"The person I'm after is connected to these strange events," Liv stated. "What if you take me on a tour of the swamp, and I explain some of what's going on?"

Al grinned. "Well, that would be just about perfect. Let me just finish with my gas, and we can be on our way."

He cleared the passenger seat for her and patted it. "Go ahead and hop in and get comfortable."

"Thanks, Al." Liv slapped her arm and wiped the dead bug on her pant leg. She was pretty certain she wasn't going to be comfortable until she was out of the hot and muggy swamp, but at least she'd made a friend, and hopefully, she'd stop the SandMan.

CHAPTER TWENTY-SIX

"Have you seen any questionable characters out here?" Liv asked as Al lowered the boat into the water. He was skilled at this, doing it without even thinking.

"Well, like I said, I've seen a lot of things out of the ordinary," he began. "Makes me think I'm losing my mind. My momma says I'm spending too much time on the water and the heat is getting to me."

Liv fanned herself since her cheeks were warm. "Although the heat does crazy things to people, I don't think that's it."

"But to answer your question, I ain't seen nobody out. It's a bit strange. There hasn't been anyone wanting to tour, which is why I'm mighty grateful for your business today, Liv."

So Zeno Dutillet was hiding. She had expected that. Liv didn't know where to start to draw him out, but she hoped she got a bright idea while they were out on the water.

Al pushed the boat out once he'd gotten the truck parked. The water was calm and a murky green color. Liv peered over the side of the boat, curious what lived in these waters.

"Okay, today we're going to be out exploring the Atchafalaya Basin," Al began, powering up the motor. "Because I use a smaller boat, we can really get into the nooks and crannies of the bayou, giving you an experience unlike any other."

Liv wanted to tell the nice guy that he didn't have to do his normal spiel, but she didn't want to tarnish his spirit, so she sat on the edge of her seat, peering intently into the dense forest that surrounded them.

"This area we're exploring is the largest contiguous forested wetland in North America," Al continued.

"How deep is this water?" Liv asked.

"It's eight to nine feet, currently."

"Is it safe to swim in?"

Al laid his hand on the throttle. "Well, sure. I've been swimming in it all my life, but I'm not sure a girl such as yourself would like it so much. There's a lot of slimy things in there and you'd for sure mess up your hair."

Liv nodded like that was a concern for her. She had no plans to go swimming, but she wanted to be prepared for just about anything.

"Are you ready to go fast?" Al asked, a dimple surfacing on his face when he grinned.

"Yes, let's do it."

The boat kicked it into high gear, speeding them across the placid water ahead. For a few minutes, they veered one way and then another, taking multiple routes through the swamp, getting deeper and deeper.

Al was right that Liv would have easily gotten lost in

these wetlands. However, he didn't know she had a phone that worked anywhere and magic that worked in most places. Still, she was strangely grateful to have this mortal with her. He had kind eyes and an easy grin, and something told her that when the little critters came out, she'd be glad he was there.

"Now, because it's almost sunset, we're going to see some animals coming out to feed," Al explained, slowing the boat down and coasting them through leaves that floated on the water.

Al dipped his hand into the water, pulling up a pile of leaves. "If you look real close, you'll notice a frog here. They, like everything in the swamp, camouflage themselves real good. You won't even be able to spot half the creatures out here unless I point them out, which is part of the fun. Spotting animals takes a trained eye."

Liv noticed the tiny frog nestled in the leaves. But in the distance, she spotted a large spider on a tree. It was easily the size of her hand.

"What's that?" she asked, pointing.

Al blinked in that direction. "Oh, you do have a good eye. That's a fishing spider. Guess why we call them that?"

Liv gulped, her skin suddenly feeling itchy. "I'm guessing because they eat fish. What about people?"

Al laughed. "Well, I think that'd be damned near impossible. And don't worry, they won't bother you unless you mess with them."

"Isn't that the rule for most things?" Liv asked as the boat floated closer to the large brown spider.

Al gave her a reluctant expression. "Sometimes."

She didn't like the uncertainty in his eyes, but she

forced a smile anyway. "I think we need to get deeper into the swamp. Can you do that? Get us as far from civilization as possible?"

Liv's instincts told her that Zeno Dutillet would want to be far from people, making it impossible for him to be found. And he'd picked the perfect place to hide.

"Oh, sure. But I'll warn you. When I've gotten deeper into the swamp lately, that's when I see things I can't explain. This place has always been strangely magical, but lately, well, it's something else entirely."

"These strange things you've seen," Liv began. "Can you expand?"

Al pointed into the distance. "I can do one better. There's one of the weird creatures now. What does that look like to you?"

Liv squinted, trying to make out the shape swimming ahead of the boat. "Is that an otter?"

The creature barked suddenly, its call echoing through the forest.

"That's what I would have thought," Al started. "I'm telling you that I rarely have seen an otter in these waters, but now I see these things all the time in these parts."

"Things?" Liv asked as Al cut the engine.

The boat floated closer to the otter, who didn't seem to be making fast progress across the water.

Al removed the necklace he was wearing and held it over the side of the boat. "Watch this."

The otter swam over immediately, water gliding over its head as it moved gracefully. When it was right underneath where Al had the necklace dangling, it poked up its head, but instead of an otter's face with dog-like eyes and whiskers, it had the features of a human child. Its rosy cheeks and blue eyes were a strange sight surrounded by the dark fur. Liv recognized it immediately as a Lutrinae. They were carnivores that had long, slim bodies, short limbs, webbed feet, sharp claws, and human faces. They were very playful and also quite mischievous, stealing shiny objects.

Right on cue, the Lutrinae grabbed Al's necklace and ducked back under the water.

"That's pretty crazy, huh?" Al asked, giving her a look of surprise. "They look just like otters, don't they?"

"Actually…" Liv drew out the word, trying to figure out how best to explain this. "There are no such things as otters."

"Huh?" Al gave her a look of disbelief. "Come again now?"

"That," she said, pointing to where the Lutrinae had popped up again, already wearing Al's necklace, "is a Lutrinae. You've seen them before, but they always appeared to be otters to you."

"Wait, you're telling me that otters have never existed but these Lu-whatevers have?"

Liv nodded. "You see, as a mortal, you've never been able to see magical creatures before. Your brain always saw them as something acceptable. However, what you're seeing now is real."

Al laughed. "You sound like you've subscribed to that silly business the President lady has been spreading. She's been telling us magic is real. Have you ever heard of anything so ridiculous?"

"But you yourself said that what you've been seeing in the swamp seems magical," Liv argued.

"Yeah, but that's just something that people say," Al countered. "I mean, that otter-thing is weird, but I was just figuring that it's a deformed species. Maybe from too much pollution."

Liv was about to argue when she felt something tug at Bellator. She spun around to find the Lutrinae trying to steal her sword. "Hey, now!" She slapped the creature's hand away.

It gave her a look of offense and slipped back under the water.

Al pulled off his hat, rubbing his head. "You telling me that's normal?"

"Yes, but I get that it's a lot to digest."

"Now, you called me a mortal," Al stated, driving the boat into a particularly dense area. The tree canopy overhead was solid, shrouding them in darkness. "What would that make you?"

Liv took a deep breath, enjoying the fresh, moist air. "I'm a magician."

The tour guide laughed. "Oh, that's what the news has been saying. Apparently, there are elves, gnomes, and all sorts. I can't tell you how many people on social media are now claiming they are related to elves or something."

Liv had heard about this. Mortals who were obsessed with what they had always thought was fantasy were now claiming they were magicians or elves. They weren't, and it was making everything really confusing, but she suspected things would get stranger before they got sorted out.

"I can prove I'm a magician," Liv said, hoping to help this guy.

He slowed the boat, grabbing a cypress branch to halt them. "I definitely want to see this. Go on, then."

Liv nodded, trying to decide what small spell she could perform to prove her point.

"Don't do it," someone said in the distance.

Al spun. Liv squinted in that direction.

"What was that?" she asked.

He nodded like it had made sense. "The swamp can make all sorts of noises that sound like chatter. That's normal. I've heard them since I was little. Branches sawing back and forth and leaves swaying in the wind sound just like someone talking."

The voice came again. "No, they don't."

Liv bounded forward, leaning over the side of the boat to get a better look. "I don't think so." She could barely make out the outline of an alligator lying on a log. He was at least five feet long and seemed to be staring straight at them.

"Isn't that an alligator?" She pointed.

"Oh, well, sure it is," Al stated. "Again, you've got a good eye."

"Yes, good eye," the alligator said, and then winked at her.

Al laughed, looking up at the canopy overhead. "Isn't it crazy the things the breeze says? When I was little, I used to imagine that gators could talk to me and would steer me in the right direction when I was lost in the bayou."

"You're welcome," the alligator chirped.

Liv glanced at Al and the alligator. "You don't hear that coming from the alligator?"

Al shook his head, pointing at the trees. "I hear the sounds of the swamp. My momma used to tell me that if a man spent too much time alone out here, he'd go crazy from the voices of the swamp. That's apparently why my daddy don't come out here anymore."

Liv nodded slowly. Even if mortals could see and hear magical creatures now, that didn't mean they *would*. It was a lot to digest.

She was about to question the talking alligator, which she'd also heard about in magical creatures. Not all alligators could speak, but the ones related to Godzilla apparently could. It was a complicated bit of history which Liv didn't know that well. However, before she could ask the alligator anything, something streaked through the woods in the distance.

"What's that?" Liv asked, pointing.

It was another boat, she realized at once.

"That's odd," Al said, recognizing it as it drifted behind a dense bit of trees. "That's one of Jeb's boats, I believe."

"The same Jeb who told me none of his boats worked?" Liv questioned.

"Well, yeah, but I didn't recognize that person on the boat as Jeb or one of his boys," Al said. "I think that guy had a black mohawk."

CHAPTER TWENTY-SEVEN

Could Spencer be following her? That seemed strange, but what were the odds that she was in the middle of nowhere and some random guy with a mohawk showed up in the same place?

Liv was about to use a cloaking spell on them when something tugged at her pocket.

She jerked her head down to once again find the Lutrinae's hand trying to dig into her cloak where she kept her Warrior ring. She shot the creature a murderous expression, and it held up its paws as if in surrender and slipped back into the water.

Al's chuckle brought her attention back up, but then something huge dropped down from the trees. Liv barely caught a glimpse of the eight long, hairy legs before it grabbed Al. He screamed as the giant spider stuck its fangs into the side of his neck, then pounced off the side of the boat and straight back up into the tree.

Liv whipped her head up, watching as the shadow of

the spider the size of a baby grand piano traversed easily overhead, disappearing into the darkness of the canopy.

"Al!" Liv yelled, realizing it would do no good. The mortal was gone. A large fishing spider had taken him.

"And he said that they only mess with you if you mess with them," Plato said, suddenly by her side.

Liv yanked Bellator from her sheath, spinning in a circle and assessing the area. "Apparently that spider thought he was a threat."

"Or someone else thinks *you're* a threat and is trying to distract you," Plato offered.

"Well, whether this is a trap or a distraction, I have to get Al back. He wouldn't even be out here if it wasn't for me."

"I agree," Plato said. "But the mortal will hopefully be okay until you can get to him."

"How do you figure?" Liv asked, revolving again and continuing to search the swamp.

"Because spiders like to wrap their prey up before they kill it."

"Thanks, but that only makes me feel slightly better," Liv said. "Spencer is out there somewhere, isn't he?"

"I don't want to bog you down with details, but yes," Plato answered.

Liv lowered her chin, giving the cat an annoyed expression. "You didn't just go there?"

"And you thought *you* were the queen of puns."

Liv shook her head.

"Spencer the one putting everyone to sleep?" the alligator said, looking right at them. There was no mistaking it. That reptile was talking.

"No. But have you seen Zeno Dutillet?" Liv asked, leaning over the boat, trying to figure out how to get closer. She was going to have to steer. Good thing she'd been paying attention while Al was driving.

"If that's the guy known as the SandMan, then I have," the alligator said, slipping into the water and swimming closer to the boat. Liv tensed, Bellator in her hands, but for some odd reason, she didn't feel like she was in danger.

"I need to know where he is," Liv stated. "And also, how do I get Al back? And yes, where is that other magician?"

"Don't swamp him with questions," Plato said.

Liv let out a long, annoyed breath.

The alligator opened its snout, a loud laugh spilling out. "I will tell you where the SandMan is if you feed me the lynx."

Liv pretended to think that over.

"What? No! No deal," Plato protested.

"Yeah, I can't let you have the cat, even if he scolds me for puns and then uses them just as poorly as me. What else can I offer you?" she asked the alligator.

"A bit of conversation," it answered at once.

"Say what?" Liv questioned.

"Well, it gets lonely out here, and I'm a naturally talkative guy, but most of the alligators out here don't speak. When I try talking to the fishermen, well, they always freak out and leave. So maybe we could have a simple conversation."

Liv gave Plato a look of disbelief.

The cat shrugged. "He could be asking for something more difficult, and talking comes easily to you. Many consider that you chat too much as it is."

"By many, do you mean, *by you?*"

Plato hung his head. "Oh, I can't top that. Worst. Pun. Ever."

"Good. Don't cross the line into my pun territory," Liv warned.

"I'm seeing a lot of talking going on, but I'm not part of this conversation," the alligator said.

"Do you have any bad puns?" Plato asked. "You and Liv can chat for days."

Liv shook her head. "What do you want to talk about?"

"Oh, my name is Smeg," the alligator said. "And I'd like to talk about antidisestablishmentarianism."

"This should be interesting," Plato said with a laugh.

Dismissing the lynx, Liv focused on Smeg. "Although I'd like to have a long conversation on withdrawing governmental support from church, I'm sort of swamped at the moment."

Smeg laughed. Plato, thankfully, stopped.

"In all seriousness, I have to get that mortal back, and I have to stop the SandMan," Liv stated.

"And then there's the guy at your back who looks ready to attack you," Smeg stated casually.

"What?" Liv barked, spinning around to find Spencer's boat had soundlessly glided up next to hers. Although he wore a considering expression and held a machete in his hands, she wasn't sure if she should attack first. He hadn't done anything yet.

"P, when were you going to tell me that a fellow Warrior was right behind me?" Liv asked from the corner of her mouth.

Honestly, I didn't sense him, which is strange, Plato answered, not out loud, but rather in her head.

"Hey, Spencer," Liv said, injecting pleasantness into her voice. "What brings you out this way?"

He didn't answer, only stared.

"So, a machete?" Liv asked as their boats drifted closer together. "That's a strange weapon for a magician."

He pulled the large knife back and flung it straight in Liv's direction. She swerved, narrowly avoiding getting hit, and it landed in the water.

Liv popped up, noticing that Plato had vanished. Spencer reached down, picking up what appeared to be a filet knife for cleaning fish. So it was going to be like this, Liv thought.

She produced a fireball and was just about to shoot at him when scurrying in the trees overhead caught her attention. Quickly Liv glanced up, catching sight of the giant spider again. It didn't appear to have Al. She worried it was coming for her this time.

"Watch out!" Smeg called from behind her.

Liv spun just in time to see Spencer throwing the knife. Without time to avoid it, Liv raised Bellator into the air and deflected the blade. This only seemed to encourage the evil warrior.

Spencer pulled up three more knives, throwing one after the other in Liv's direction. She had to spin her large sword at lightning speed to deflect all the weapons before they hit her.

She was nearly knocked off-balance when their boats bumped. Spencer jumped up like a spider and landed beside her in Al's boat. He had two short blades in his hands and a menace that could burn on his face.

Liv stepped to the side, holding Bellator firmly and trying to figure out how best to attack. It felt strange to attack this warrior even if she had been provoked. He was a Sinclair, though, she told herself.

"Why did you come after me?" Liv asked him, twirling Bellator.

"Because," he said simply.

Liv rolled her eyes. "Why do people think that is a sufficient response to a question?"

"You must be stopped," he continued.

"Now we're getting somewhere," Liv stated. "Who told you I must be stopped?"

Spencer didn't answer this time. Instead, he lunged at her, trying to stab with the small blade. Liv bowed her body to avoid the attack.

She knew what had to happen next, but the idea of killing another Sinclair was repellent to her. However, she had to defend herself. With speed supplied to her by Bellator, she brought the sword up and around. It seemed to know where its target was. The blade moved swiftly through the air, slicing cleanly through the magician before her.

Too cleanly, actually.

He froze. His mouth opened. Liv looked between the clean cut she'd made through his abdomen and his look of disbelief, wondering if she should apologize. Then, before her eyes, Spencer turned to dust, crumbling before a gust of wind knocked him out of the boat, spreading him across the water.

CHAPTER TWENTY-EIGHT

Frantically, Liv spun one way and then the other, looking for the real Spencer. She heard frogs croaking and ducks quacking, but there was no sign of the actual magician.

"How was he there and then not?" she wondered as his boat drifted away.

"He wasn't real," Plato said, reappearing at Liv's side.

"Oh, look, my fair-weather friend has returned," she grumbled, taking the wheel of the boat. It was up to her to head them in the right direction.

"I didn't sense him at your back because he wasn't real," Plato stated.

"I don't understand what that means," Liv argued, steering the boat into a denser part of the swamp. She had to duck to avoid hitting her head on low branches.

"Well, he could hold a sword and drive a boat, so he was real enough," Plato began, "but I got the impression that he was about as real as the suits of armor."

"So he was possessed?" Liv asked, remembering how Rooster had made the suits of armor come alive.

"Well, yes and no. His body dissolved when you stabbed him, so I think he was more of an illusion."

"An illusion?" Liv asked. "Those can do actual things?"

Plato nodded. "A very powerful illusionist can make their illusions do just about anything. But the more they have to do, the harder it is."

"So the real Spencer isn't real, or the one I slew just now wasn't? Or both?" Liv asked, absolutely confused.

"I'm not sure, exactly," Plato stated honestly.

Liv sighed. "This is confusing."

"Where are you going?" Plato asked.

"I don't know. I was hoping to find Smeg. I thought I saw him retreat this way."

Plato nodded in the direction of some water covered in greenery. "I think I saw an alligator over there, but it's hard to know if it was Chatty Cathy or not."

Liv decided to take her chances, steering the boat over there. The branches were still low in this area, and she was nearly poked in the face by a twig or two as she passed.

For ten minutes, they drifted in silence, looking for signs of the alligator known as Smeg. The smell of tree sap and blood was strangely strong in the air. Cautiously, Liv searched the waters, hoping not to find Al dead somewhere nearby. He couldn't be. She had to save him. Somehow.

She saw a head pop out of the water and jumped up. It was an alligator! "Smeg," she called, hitting her head on a branch when she nearly hopped out of the boat with excitement.

The alligator didn't grin at her or start talking. Instead, it ducked back under the surface of the water and swam away.

Liv deflated. "So it wasn't Smeg."

She didn't have long to feel sorry for herself, because immediately she heard buzzing overhead. With a tentative glance up, she noticed a few dozen things starting to swarm above her head. She crouched and just caught the thing she'd hit with her head in her peripheral vision. It was a hornet's nest!

The swarm was on her, a couple having already stung her head. Liv swept her arms through the air, but she knew that wouldn't work. Without a moment of hesitation, she dove straight over the side of the boat into the murky waters of the swamp.

It was cold, and she was weighed down from Bellator. Still, she stayed down under the surface of the water, blinking up and watching as the swarm of angry hornets circled overhead, looking to punish whoever had hit their nest.

Knowing she couldn't hold her breath for long, Liv found the side of the boat and began pushing it through the thick water of the bayou. She was hyper-aware that there had been an alligator close by just before she jumped, but she remained underwater, propelling the boat forward and ignoring little bites she got on her shins and ankles.

When she couldn't hold her breath any longer, Liv decided it was safe to come up for air. She took a giant breath when her head popped up. Water weeds and other strange plants were covering her head and shoulders.

Seeing that the swarm was gone, she tried to figure out

how to climb back into the boat without pulling it over. She was just about to make her first attempt when the smell of blood hit her senses again.

She pushed away some leaves that were bumping into her back, kicking her legs underneath her. The smell of blood was disconcerting, but her main objective was to get back into the boat.

Again the plants rocked into her shoulder. Nearly offended by the plants that wouldn't give her freedom, she jerked around.

A scream shot out of her mouth, making a flock of birds rise from the trees. A man who strangely looked just like Jeb was floating in the water beside her, his eyes open and his mouth full of disgusting bugs. He was missing a leg or two, and maybe an arm, Liv noticed as she pushed the boat away, kicking after it. When she was a good distance away, she clambered over the side, grateful that she didn't capsize it.

Panting from adrenaline and fear, she stared over the edge of the boat at the man floating dead in the swamp.

Beside her, Plato appeared. "This is probably a bad time…"

Liv gave him a furious stare, conscious that she had all sorts of plant life dripping from her body and that she was soaked through. "What?"

He gave her his best Cheshire Cat grin. "You've got something in your hair."

CHAPTER TWENTY-NINE

Liv pulled a clump of soggy plants from the pocket of her cape and tossed it over the side of the boat. Her hair was a disaster, she smelled like rotting fish, and she had been drifting through the swamp for another ten minutes, unable to locate the alligator known as Smeg.

The sun would be going down soon. They were running out of time. And the longer Al was gone, the more Liv worried about his fate. He must be really frightened.

"Who killed Jeb?" Liv asked. "Was it Spencer?"

"And when?" Plato asked. "That body looks to have been dead for a while, but you just spoke to him earlier today."

"Good point," Liv said, musing on the idea. "There is definitely something fishy going on here."

"I'm considering morphing into another form and throwing you overboard," Plato threatened.

"You wouldn't dare," Liv fired back, but bolted upright with a sudden realization. "Hey, Plato. You want to help, right?"

"Not really," he answered. "It's sort of against my DNA, but sometimes I accidentally do it, or that's how you perceive it."

"Well, are you okay with me using you for bait?"

Plato's head snapped to the side, his green eyes bulging. "Say what?"

Liv leaned down and picked the feline up. "Just tell me if this isn't okay."

He grunted mildly. "It's a bit disgraceful, but I guess."

"I would have preferred it if you had put up a bit more of a fight about this," Liv said, lowering the lynx toward the surface of the water.

"Don't you know that I know that?" Plato said.

"And you refuse to give me satisfaction," Liv realized.

"Exactly," he said as Liv dipped his lower half under the murky water, holding it there for a few minutes.

"I guess you're overdue for a bath." She smiled at him, enjoying the opportunity to turn the tables.

"I just had a bath," he argued.

"While I was battling suits of armor," she refuted. "Why in the world did you pick that as a time to bathe and sleep rather than just disappearing as usual?"

"Well, I didn't feel any danger from Rooster, firstly," he explained. "And I'm starting to regret hiding at every instance."

"Really?" Liv asked.

"Really," he answered. "I don't get to share certain moments, and that used to not bother me, but now it's starting to get to me."

"Why?" Liv asked, skeptically.

Plato turned his head to the side, not appearing like he wanted to answer the question.

"Is this a part of the bigger secret?" Liv asked.

"Yeah, maybe, but I think we should focus more on the fact that something is swimming and more importantly *quickly* swimming my way, about to eat my butt," Plato said, his voice frantic.

"Just let me know when I'm almost out of time, and I'll pull you up," Liv said.

"The time is upon us!" Plato yelled.

Liv jerked him into the air, holding him high just as Smeg jumped, chomping after the dangling tail.

Liv tossed the lynx into the safety of the boat and leaned forward. "So, Smeg, are you ready to have a long convo?"

The alligator paddled around, facing her. "Absolutely. What are we talking about?"

"Sure, I was thinking I could tell you about the plot of a video game I played recently," Liv began.

"No!" Smeg yelled. "I'll just lead you to the SandMan. Please don't put me through that torture."

"Oh, but there's this one guy, and he learns he has powers of the turkey but knows he can do better, so he goes to this other guy, who is going to help him if he can prove his worth through—"

"Please, no!" Smeg yelled. "I want real conversation. I will do anything to avoid talking about video game storylines."

"Sounds good," Liv stated. "How about you tell me the whereabouts of the SandMan, then we can talk about politics and religion and whatever else you'd like."

Happily, the alligator swam beside the boat, leading the way. "This sounds perfect to me, Liv. What do you think about global warming? I for one have noticed some changes, but I've been around for a very long time, so how am I to know?"

CHAPTER THIRTY

Smeg led them through veils of plants, down inlets that Liv was sure the boat couldn't navigate, and into a forest unlike any she'd ever experienced.

The trees seemed to sway. Several times she noticed something move at the corner of her vision. Every time she turned, though, there was nothing there. Well, there were trees and water and plants and gross bugs, but nothing out of the ordinary.

She could have sworn she'd seen faces on the trees. Several times, she thought she caught one grinning at her, but after closer inspection, the trunk just had regular knobs and branches that in the light looked like a face.

"He's just past this merman's house," Smeg said, indicating with his snout what Liv thought was a beaver's dam.

"That's a merman's house?" Liv asked, realizing that even as a magician, she knew little about the world. It wasn't what it seemed, and she had much to learn.

"Yes, but he isn't home right now," Smeg began. "His

name is Cyrus, and he works as a chef at a local seafood place in town."

"The commute must be a bitch," Liv observed, realizing they were at least an hour from the dock where they had started.

"Oh, mermen are incredibly fast swimmers. It doesn't take him long to get home, which could be bad for you if he returns while you're here. He doesn't take kindly to strangers in his territory, which is why he lives out here."

"But the SandMan is out here," Liv pointed out.

"Yes, but he keeps to himself, and then there's that whole being invincible thing," Smeg explained. "Cyrus was real angry when the SandMan took up residence here. He threw an entire arsenal of tridents at him, but it did zero good. Then he gave up. But he might be getting mad again since he says all his customers keep falling asleep."

This didn't make Liv feel any more confident about stopping Zeno Dutillet. She pulled from her pocket the story Papa Creola had given her. It was, of course, soaked through from her fall into the swamp. The writing was smudged so badly that she could hardly make out the words.

"Oh no," Liv said, feeling suddenly hopeless. "What am I supposed to do?"

"Well, you do have Father Time on speed dial," Plato suggested.

Liv gave him a curious look. "Did you just make a reference from 1990?"

"I'm timeless, what can I say?" he said proudly.

Liv pulled her phone from her pocket, grateful she had service and that the device was waterproof, thanks to

Alicia's magic tech skills. There were already a few messages from Papa Creola with different timestamps. She should have known.

They read:

Don't fall into the swamp 5:03 pm

Okay, you fell into the swamp. Not good. 5:20 pm

You're going to need a new story. 5:21 pm

Liv typed out a message to him. **Can you please send me one?**

Before she could send it, he sent a message.

No. 5:55 pm

With a loud sigh, she rolled her eyes.

Simply make up your own bedtime story to put Zeno Dutillet to sleep. 5:55 pm

Liv just stared at the screen, knowing there had to be more.

But it has to be a new story. One that has never been told before. Ever. 5:55 pm

And there it was, she thought. Of course, she had to make the SandMan sit and listen to her tell a tale, and it needed to be one that no one had ever heard before.

Papa Creola sent another message.

I'll be in touch after you put him to sleep. 5:56 pm

Liv's chest lightened with hope. That had to mean that she would be successful.

Another message came through.

Well, if you put him to sleep. Those events aren't clear. 5:56 pm

She deflated again, giving Plato a sideways look. "Any bright ideas on new stories that have never been told before?"

"Well, how about one where everyone mysteriously disappears on a battlecruiser, and these two misfits have to find them? Oh, wait. That one won't work. How about one about a girl with blue hair who learns she's half-mortal and half-witch? Never mind. I think I've read that one too." He shrugged. "I think there's only one viable option."

"I quit this Warrior business and see if Cyrus will hire me to wash dishes at the seafood restaurant?" Liv asked.

Plato shook his head. "The only story you can tell that no one has ever heard is yours."

"I'm supposed to tell Zeno Dutillet the story of my life?"

"Well, I've been there for most of it, and there's not another story quite like it," Plato reasoned.

"But that will take forever," Liv stated.

"Leave out the fluff," Plato offered. "That's the key to a good story. Oh, and you have to share all the gruesome details. The stuff you don't like to think about."

"So I have to share my deepest, darkest secrets with the SandMan?" she asked in disbelief.

Plato shrugged again, noncommittally. "If you want to put him to sleep." A moment later, he added, "And you'll need to remember the story in its entirety since that will be what will bind him to sleep."

"Wouldn't it be better to lose the story so no one can ever wake him again?" she questioned.

Plato shook his head. "The story will only work to put him to sleep if it's documented. All good bedtime stories eventually end up in a book."

Liv closed her eyes, thinking of her life, letting all the details spill into her consciousness. She smiled when she saw her parents, and she nearly cried when she saw herself leaving the House after their deaths. Something felt ready to bound out of her chest when she defeated Adler Sinclair, releasing mortals. It was only a minute, but during that time, she allowed the events of her life to play across her mind.

With a strange, creative confidence she'd never known, fueled more by instinct than ever before, she held out her hand. A small leather-bound book appeared.

It was compact and had no pictures, but it was full of stories that had never been told before.

It was the story of Liv Beaufont's life.

CHAPTER THIRTY-ONE

The alligator, leading the way, stopped without warning, making Liv have to circle around to where he was. He was looking at the trees overhead.

"Why did we stop?" Liv asked.

"We are here. The SandMan is up there," Smeg explained.

Liv glared up, squinting in the darkness. At first, she didn't see anything but leaves and branches. Then the shadows arranged themselves just right so that she could make out the faint outline of a man lounging in a hammock slung between two trees.

"Is he sleeping?" Liv wondered, but just then she heard a faint whistle from the figure. He reached back, pushing against the tree by his head, making the hammock sway more.

When he pulled his hand back, Liv noticed that he had a small knife and was whittling something.

"Do you think I could ask him to come down here so I can tell him my story?" Liv asked Plato.

"I'm doubtful he'll be so accommodating."

"Well, maybe I can shout it from here," Liv suggested.

"But bedtime stories are supposed to be told in a pleasant manner," Plato stated. "Not shouted from a swamp boat."

Liv huffed. "Fine. I guess I'm climbing."

Plato bounded out of the boat gracefully, landing on a limb of a tree. In a matter of seconds, he was up the large cypress. After a moment, he glanced down at Liv. "Are you coming?"

She nodded, wishing she had the agility of a cat. That gave her an idea, one that she hoped she wouldn't come to regret.

Pointing at herself, Liv muttered a very complicated incantation. If she got it wrong, she would forever be transformed.

She shrank immediately. It felt like she'd suddenly been ground up, stuck into a coffee can, and had a tight lid stuck onto her. She wasn't a cup of Joe, though. Liv had turned herself into a cat. An all-black one.

Testing her legs, she jumped onto the side of the boat.

Smeg popped out of the water, his eyes large. "Oh, yum!"

Liv wanted to tell him to back off, but she didn't have the ability to speak. That would require a stronger trans-figuration. Instead, she bounded off the boat, finding her balance easily.

Not as gracefully as Plato, she climbed the tree.

"I never thought I'd see the day," Plato said, staring down at her with an amused expression.

He should have been happy she couldn't speak, Liv

thought as she neared where Zeno Dutillet was swinging in his hammock, whistling loudly and whittling.

She wasn't far from him when the whistling stopped. He sat upright, staring over the side of the hammock. Now that she was closer, she noticed that he had skin the color of molasses and not a single wrinkle on his face.

"Who goes there?" he called over the side of the hammock, his Southern accent making him sound like he was singing. "Those who show up unexpected aren't welcome."

Liv realized then how genius it had been to transform into a cat. Zeno Dutillet couldn't sense her entirely. That wasn't going to last for long, though.

She went unnoticed in her all-black form as she jumped onto the branch beside his hammock. Then she made the mistake of looking down. Liv didn't realize how far she'd climbed. They were at least two stories up, the boat and Smeg floating in the growing darkness below.

As she drew in a breath, she hoped the reverse transformation went smoothly. This time it felt like she'd been brewed, poured into a cup, and stirred. Coffee went through strange things, and Liv had no idea why transfigurations mirrored it so much. Curious, for sure.

Zeno Dutillet's eyes widened at the sight of her. "Well, if it ain't Olivia Beaufont. And here I thought it would be some unwanted visitor who would try to put me back to sleep. You know, you and I are related through distant cousins."

She settled cautiously onto the branch where she stood and smiled. "I didn't know that. How have you been?"

He stretched his arms overhead and yawned. "I'm fairly

good. The merman leaves me alone, which is nice. And I'm finally getting my strength back. Each mortal that slips into forever sleep helps me get back to normal."

Liv nodded like she was interested in this bit of knowledge and slipped the small book out of her pocket.

The smile on Zeno Dutillet's face faded. "What you got there, Cousin Beaufont?"

"Oh, this?" Liv said innocently. "It's nothing."

The hammock began to rock as Zeno Dutillet kicked his legs back and forth. "And here I thought you came to keep me company."

"I did," Liv argued. "I'm going to read you a story." She cracked open the book, enjoying the scent of fresh pages. Her eyes widened at the first sentence on the page.

"Once upon a time, a girl who had the power to change everything was born. Whether she would was yet to be determined," she read, her voice catching on the words. She'd thought of the story, but didn't know how it would weave together. As she read, her throat caught from the poetry of the words of her story.

"Oh, no, you don't, Cousin Beaufont," Zeno Dutillet said, swinging more furiously. The trees began to screech from the force of the hammock moving.

"In every person's life, there is that rare and distinct moment when they doubt their loyalties," Liv continued reading, speeding through the words, but also trying to soak them in. This was her tale, and yet, she wanted to know how it ended. Would there be a happy ending? Would Liv Beaufont survive? Would she actually change everything for the better?

"I'm afraid this is when I've got to take my leave," Zeno Dutillet stated. "This family reunion is over."

He bounded out of the hammock, gracefully falling through the air. With a soft thud, he landed in a crouch in the boat below, making it sink momentarily.

When Zeno Dutillet regained his balance, he glanced up, waving at Liv. "It's been nice seeing you, Cousin Beaufont, but I've got to go. I hope you don't mind if I borrow your boat."

CHAPTER THIRTY-TWO

"Firstly, I do mind," Liv yelled down at the SandMan. "And it's not my boat."

He shrugged. "Well, I'd say I was gonna return it, but I've got no plans to do that."

Liv stood and peered down at Zeno Dutillet far below.

"I really hope I don't end up in the swamp again." She held her breath and took the plunge.

Her heart met her throat as she free-fell, not doing it quite as gracefully as her supposed cousin. She had to work to keep her hands pressed tight to her body since the wind seemed to want to make them flail around.

Liv knew that if she ended up in the swamp again, the story of her life would be cut short and she'd be out of options. And then there was the very real option that Zeno would have the boat moved before her fall was complete. He appeared to be trying to get the boat running, but didn't seem to understand how it worked.

With a loud thud, Liv landed in the middle of the boat,

nearly toppling over the side. She threw her balance in the opposite direction, trying to compensate as the boat teetered from side to side.

"Dagnabit!" Zeno Dutillet yelled, staring at the controls of the boat. "How does this blasted thing work?"

Liv took a deep breath and raised the book again, having to squint to read in the growing darkness.

Zeno Dutillet blinked like sleep was suddenly overtaking him. Then his eyes brightened when he saw the key in the ignition. He turned it, and the motor started. Liv began to read faster.

"Now, how do I get this thing going?" Zeno Dutillet asked, turning his head to the side and studying the controls.

Liv was speeding over the words, hardly opening her mouth to speak. She flipped the pages with such a force that they nearly ripped several times.

"Cousin Beaufont, you're not finishing that story," the SandMan threatened. "I'm sure you're a good magician, but we're about to part ways."

"After all these years, they'd finally found her," Liv read, completely engrossed in her own story. "There would be no running. No more hiding. It was time she faced her past."

"It's a fine story," Zeno Dutillet said, yawning, his shoulders slumping slightly. "But I ain't going back to sleep. There's so much of the world I need to see. So much I've missed. I don't even know how technology works."

Liv continued, nearly choking up several times.

His face brightened when he figured out how the

throttle worked. He wrapped his hand around it, pressed a button, and jerked it all the way up. The boat took off like a bullet, throwing Liv down, the book sliding to the other side of the boat.

CHAPTER THIRTY-THREE

The boat took a hard turn, throwing Liv's shoulder into the side. Her head smashed into one of the seats and Bellator pinched into her side. She felt like a single sardine being knocked around inside a tin.

"I do apologize, Cousin Beaufont! Please don't take offense. You've got your mission, and I've got mine."

Liv had to give it to Zeno Dutillet. He had manners and class. She almost didn't want to be angry with him. Then her face smacked into a tackle box that had come loose from under one of the seats and she lost her good will toward her long-lost cousin.

Another quick turn sent Liv rolling to the other side of the boat, the book sliding past her. She reached for it, but it was just out of her grasp.

Zeno Dutillet, seeing what she was trying to do, threw the boat into reverse, sending Liv and the book rolling toward the bow.

The book knocked into the SandMan's foot. He grinned, stomping down on it.

Liv narrowed her eyes at the man before her. "And now it's my turn to apologize, Cousin Dutillet."

Confusion made his kind expression drop.

She pointed her finger at his pant leg, and it erupted in fire. Immediately, he jumped off the book, leaning over the side of the boat and splashing water on his leg to extinguish the flames.

"Oh, for Pete's sake, this was my best pair of pants, and now look what you've done to them," he complained.

It had worked, though and Liv extended her hand, bringing the book soaring into her outstretched fingers.

Zeno Dutillet's eyes widened with horror when she opened the book again, looking for where she'd left off.

"Oh, no, you don't," he said, dowsing his pants once more for good measure. "I've got no idea why you want me to sleep. I only affect mortals, not you."

"Mortals count," Liv said, her eyes honing in on the right place on the page. "The blue eyes that looked up at Liv made her knees weak. How had she missed Sophia Beaufont so much and never realized it until that moment?

Zeno Dutillet shook his head as if trying to shake away sleep. He threw his hand onto the throttle again, sending the boat speeding through the narrow channels of the swamp. It was almost dark now, and harder to see where they were going. As the boat's speed ramped up, Liv had a hard time keeping the pages from rippling in the wind. Still she continued to read.

The SandMan cranked the wheel hard to the right, making the boat spin in place, doing a one hundred and eighty-degree turn.

Liv fell back, her spine taking an assault from the seat

she hit, but thankfully she kept hold of the book. Still, the fall had knocked the wind out of her, making her unable to speak.

"Yeehaw! I forgot how good it feels to be awake!" Zeno Dutillet yelled. "I'm obliged to you for reminding me of the fun to be had out in the world, Cousin Beaufont."

Liv remained sitting, knocking her fist into her chest to try to get her voice back. "You're welcome."

He cupped his ear. "You'll have to speak up if you want me to hear you. I can't hear over the wind!"

The boat was at full speed now, making Liv feel that her cheeks were flags in the wind. Her hair assaulted her face, and it was nearly impossible to make out the words on the page. But she didn't have much more left. Only a few paragraphs.

Pushing to her feet, she tried to maintain her balance. Zeno Dutillet cast a worried look over his shoulder. Sensing that he was about to send the boat into another spin, she used all her remaining focus and shot a paralyzing spell at him. The look on his face spoke of how insulted he was by the tactic. He couldn't so much as speak, but Liv knew she had only a few seconds until it wore off. Paralyzing spells were tough, and doing one on an ancient being such as the SandMan was incredibly difficult to maintain.

As the boat continued to speed blindly through the swamp, Liv lifted the book up, reading as fast as she could. She only had three more sentences left when Zeno Dutillet's eye started to twitch. He was breaking free of the spell.

His hand flexed by his side. She rushed over the words, barely breathing as she spoke.

He opened his mouth. Shook his head. "Oh, no, you don't, Cousin Beaufont." His hand reached for the throttle.

Liv spoke the final words as if they were only one: "The truth that binds all things is the ultimate way to protect magic, but first, it must be discovered."

The SandMan smiled. Winked at her. Liv didn't know if it had worked or not. Maybe she had missed a word or sentence or page in her haste. All Zeno had to do was pull down on the throttle and she'd be sent overboard.

Liv held her breath, knowing there was little she could do at this point.

Zeno Dutillet's eyes fluttered shut. "I'm sorry it had to go this way, Cousin Beaufont. I really wanted to like you."

And then he fell with a thump on the floor of the boat, snoring as loud as the bullfrogs in the swamp of the Atchafalaya Basin.

CHAPTER THIRTY-FOUR

Liv wasn't granted a single second to celebrate. She whipped her head up to see they were headed straight for a huge cypress tree.

She lunged over the sleeping man's body, jerking the wheel to the right, narrowly missing tree but plowing into a ton of foliage on top of the water. Pushing the throttle back down, she slowed the boat. The engine choked like it was having problems.

"I think the propeller is tangled up," Plato said, at her side again.

She nodded, throwing the boat into reverse, hoping to expel all the stuff she'd run the boat through. When she'd released enough of it that the boat seemed to get on okay again, Liv brought it to a halt, finally allowing herself to take a breath.

"So, looks like you did it," Plato said, running his gaze over the sleeping man on the floor of the boat.

"Barely," she stated with gratitude.

"Barely counts in this business.

Liv's phone chimed in her pocket. She pulled it out, finding a message from Papa Creola.

The SandMan won't stay asleep long.

Liv growled. "Of course, he won't."

Another message came through from Father Time.

You have roughly twenty minutes before he's back awake.

"Twenty minutes!" Liv yelled. "What the hell? All things I could have been told before."

It was better this way, Papa Creola texted a second later.

"This guy!" Liv said, looking at Plato for sympathy.

Another message came through. **You must find a mortal to stand guard over the SandMan. Give them the book, and once they agree to the task, he will sleep until awakened again.**

Liv looked around the almost-dark swamp. Glowing eyes blinked at her through the trees. "Oh, just find a mortal in twenty minutes. That shouldn't be hard...but wait, I'm in the middle of nowhere."

"I know of a mortal who's maybe close by," Plato offered.

How could Liv have forgotten about Al? She rejoiced. "Of course. And I need to rescue him anyway."

Her phone dinged again. She glanced at it. **This mortal and his relatives will be charged with guarding over the SandMan forever. It is not an easy task and will make them enemies to some who dare to wake him. The mortal you choose must know this before consenting.**

Liv nodded. "Yes, I should have expected this."

"So you have twenty minutes to find Al," Plato said.

The phone chimed again. Liv rolled her eyes as she brought it up to read the message. **Nineteen minutes.**

"Oh, that man…" Liv stated with another growl. "If he weren't so powerful, I'd—"

The chime of her phone interrupted her. **You'd what?**

I'd put everything on the top shelf in your office and walk away.

"He can shape-shift, you know," Plato reminded her.

"Yeah, I know," she said, thinking of when Papa Creola had changed into a fae at Rudolf's wedding. "Anyway, I don't have time to think of a proper insult. I have nineteen or eighteen minutes to save poor Al. But I don't even know where the giant, deranged spider took him."

She glanced down at her phone, wondering if Papa Creola wanted to offer any input on this one. Apparently, he didn't.

"Well, you can use a tracking spell," Plato suggested.

"Yeah, but I'll need something of Al's," Liv said, feeling defeated already. Then she perked up. "Oh, this is his boat."

"Let's hope so, or the tracking spell will lead you to whoever it legally belongs to," Plato offered.

Liv had to take the chance that this was Al's boat and not his momma's or his daddy's. She closed her eyes, touching the side of the metal boat and repeated the spell several times. She was going to run through it once more for good measure, but Plato interrupted her.

"Liv," he said tentatively.

Her eyes popped open, and she saw a trail of gold dust

snaking over the swamp before her. That was the path to Al. All she had to do was follow it. And hope that he was still alive. And defeat a giant spider.

No biggie.

CHAPTER THIRTY-FIVE

Using a silencing spell on the motor of the boat, she steered it through the swamp. When the trail of gold dust ran up the side of a tree, Liv knew it was time to tie up and start climbing.

She looked up at the canopy overhead, seeing the golden light surrounding a large object. That had to be Al.

She was really tired of climbing trees but mostly tired of falling from them. However, time was running out.

Morphing into her cat form, Liv scaled to the top of the trees until she was face to face with a giant white cocooned Al. His face was sticking out one end and his feet the other. His eyes widened in confusion at the sight of the black cat.

"Hey, little kitty, can you help me?" he said, his voice vibrating with fear. The web around him shook as if it were about to fall down at any moment.

Liv changed back into her normal form, making Al's eyes nearly pop out of his head.

"Wow! How did you do that?"

"Magic," Liv said, looking around for the spider or an easy way of releasing Al.

"I'm so grateful you came after me," he said in a rush. "I would have passed out from terror, except that I'm strangely more awake than I've ever been."

"My fault," Liv admitted, pulling Bellator from her side. "Sorry about that."

She was just about to slice through the webbing holding Al hostage when something shook the branch where she was standing.

Liv closed her eyes for a half-beat, knowing exactly what was at her back.

Twirling Bellator to the side, she pivoted, careful to keep her balance. Staring at her with its menacing eyes was a large fishing spider. It didn't appear the least bit happy to see her.

With its long legs on multiple branches, it scuttled forward.

Time was running out. Liv needed to get Al to safety. She threw the first attack, spinning Bellator up and around and straight at the body of the spider. Two of its legs came out of nowhere, deflecting the attack.

Liv nearly fell off the branch but managed to save herself. Again she swung her sword, not directing it but rather allowing Bellator to lead the way. It connected, slicing off one of the legs cleanly.

The spider screamed as it reeled. Liv took this opportunity to wheel around and try to slice through Al's ties. His eyes told her she had run out of time. Something swept her legs, making Bellator slice through part of the web. Simultaneously, Liv fell down on the branch, just as Al plummeted toward the water, still bound by the web.

A loud splash told her he'd fallen into the swamp. He'd drown if she didn't help since he was unable to swim with his arms and legs constrained.

Liv rolled over on her back, the large spider bearing down on her, its fangs dangerously close to her throat. She made a note that when she got home, all the "roommate" spiders were getting kicked out. If she never saw another spider for the rest of her life, that would be just fine.

Liv readjusted Bellator in her hands. Not because she had any bright ideas, but because it seemed to be telling her that.

The spider clamped its legs down on the lower half of her body, and a thread of silk shot out of its mouth as it began to bind her to the branch where she lay. It was working fast. Al was under the water. She was out of options.

There is still one more, Bellator seemed to say in her mind.

And because she was bonded to the giant-forged blade, she felt her arm moving without her intention to do so. In a brilliant show of power, the hand holding Bellator shot up and pushed the sword through the center of the spider, stabbing it all the way through, killing it at once. The beast screamed, making the trees shake.

Knowing she didn't have a second to spare, Liv broke out of the bonds the spider was putting on her and threw the monster to the side. It fell through the trees, catching on several branches before hitting the swamp.

As she'd done several times before, she shrank Bellator to a smaller size and then dove straight into the water below. The murky water of the swamp was dark. Finding Al would be difficult.

Twice she jerked around, looking for any sign of the mortal. She was just about to come up for air when she noticed something. It was the white glow of the spider's silk binding him. Liv kicked hard in that direction, and his face swam into view. Bubbles were spilling from his mouth. He appeared to be trying to break free, but the thread was too thick.

Liv pushed harder, making up the distance fast. She was on him in a moment, her arm around his neck, pulling him up to the surface of the water. He let out a huge gasp of relief when they were into the fresh air, drinking in oxygen.

Even though it was awkward, Liv went straight to work cutting the threads around Al. It didn't take long, but she knew every second counted. The boat was not far, only about ten yards away.

"Can you swim?" Liv asked him when he was free.

Looking totally disoriented, he sort of nodded.

"Come on, we have to get to the boat fast," she stated.

"You didn't get the spider," he said, his voice shaking.

"No, I totally did. But we don't have much time. Go!" she yelled, swimming fast for the boat. She climbed over the side when she arrived, then reached back over to help Al into his boat. He nearly jumped back out when he saw the man sleeping at the bow.

"Whoa! Is that your criminal?" Al asked.

Liv put Bellator away and pulled out the book she'd thankfully left in the boat. It was dry and intact. "This is the SandMan, Al. And I have a very important mission for you, but you have to accept it of your own accord."

When Liv was done explaining the situation to the mortal, he merely stood looking between her and Zeno Dutillet several times. "Where am I supposed to keep him?"

Liv wanted to laugh. It was a good logistical question, but she needed an answer. "It doesn't matter. Just keep him close. I believe the magic will protect him from most seeing him, but like I said, his presence will put you and your children's children in danger."

"But if he's ever woken up, then all mortals will die, won't they?" Al asked.

Liv nodded. "Will you please accept this challenge, accepting this burden for you and yours for all of time?"

He didn't even think for a moment before holding out his hand. "I, Albert Flournoy the Second, accept this, not as a burden, but rather as an honor."

Liv laid the book with the story of part of her life in his outstretched hand. The book glowed for a moment before fading back to its normal appearance. "Thank you, Al."

He smiled, looking around at the swamp. "I think it's time I get you and my permanent houseguest home. Momma will be worried sick about me."

Liv agreed, taking what felt like the first replenishing breath all day.

When they were back at the docks, Liv helped Al put Zeno Dutillet's body in the back of his truck. While he was busy covering the sleeping man, Liv made a few enhancements to Al's boat. Some were changes that John had taught her, like how to tune up a motor—using her magic, of course. The others were things Alicia had taught her using magic tech. Those two could save the world with their brilliance if they bonded together, Liv thought, standing back to admire her handiwork.

"I think that about does it," Al said, then stopped suddenly. "My boat."

Liv spun to face him, an unsure grin on her face. "Is that okay? I hope I didn't overstep."

He shook his head in disbelief. "She looks better than brand new. I'll get a ton more swamp tours now, and I don't have to pay for those repairs she's been needing."

"So you like it?" Liv asked, gratefully.

"Liv, I absolutely love it," Al said. "But there's one thing I still don't get."

Liv regarded the mortal, the nearby streetlamp providing most of the light to see him by.

"Magic is really real, isn't it?" he asked.

Liv nodded. "Yes. It always has been, but you're seeing it for the first time. Some really bad men had mortals spelled, but they are gone now."

"Yes, that's what you said," Al stated, pulling off his cap and tousling his hair. "But if they are gone, who woke Zeno Dutillet?"

Liv nodded. "Who, indeed?"

"Well, you're the detective, and I suspect you'll figure it out," he said, pointing to his truck. "Can I offer you a ride back to town?"

Liv shook her head. "No, I've got other transportation."

Then she created a portal home, desperately wanting a bath.

Al's mouth opened wide with disbelief. "Holy Mother of God! That's a real-life magic transport, isn't it?"

Liv nodded. "It sure is. Good luck, Al Flournoy. I hope we never meet again because that will mean you and Zeno Dutillet are safe."

CHAPTER THIRTY-SIX

As soon as Liv entered the Chamber of the Tree inside the House of Fourteen, she whipped out Bellator.

Each of the council members stirred to attention, their eyes on her. Lorenzo coughed uncomfortably. Kayla narrowed her dark eyes.

Haro leaned forward. "Warrior Beaufont, is everything okay?"

"No, everything isn't all right," she said, pointing her sword at the figure of Spencer Sinclair. "That's why I'm holding a freaking sword inside this chamber."

Stefan, seeing the look in her eyes, pulled his own sword, ready to join the fight even though he didn't know what it was about. Beside him, Trudy tensed, uncertainty on her face.

Spencer held up his hands, shaking his head. "I don't know what this is about."

"I killed you," Liv stated firmly.

"You what?" Lorenzo questioned.

"Well, it wasn't Spencer," Liv explained, holding Bellator firm. "It was an illusion."

"Warrior Beaufont, will you please lower the sword while we get to the bottom of this?" Haro asked.

Liv glanced at Akio beside her, who gave her an encouraging look. Because she trusted him, she brought Bellator down. Stefan followed suit.

"Now, will you please explain why you would kill a fellow warrior?" Hester asked.

Liv's eyes darted to the white tiger and the black crow that approached from opposite sides of the room. They settled down in front of the council, blinking with interest at her. "Because he came after me while I was on a case for Father Time. He had a machete and attacked me."

Spencer laughed, pulling back his cloak to reveal a long sword. "Why would I carry a machete when I have this?"

Liv narrowed her eyes at the guy with the mohawk and disingenuous smile. "I don't know, nor do I know why you came after me. I also don't know if you're real. You could be another illusion."

"Are you quite certain the Spencer you killed was an illusion?" Clark asked.

Liv rolled her eyes at her brother. "Yes. When he turned to ash and floated away, I was pretty certain he wasn't a real man."

"Now she's insulting my brother, after nearly attacking him," Kayla complained.

More than anything, Liv wanted to attack Spencer to see if he was real. However, she restrained herself.

"Warrior DeVries," Clark said, turning his attention to

Trudy. "You were about to give us a report. Was Spencer with you during your last case?"

Trudy nodded. "Yes, the entire time."

"Is it possible that someone created an illusion of Spencer to come after Warrior Beaufont?" Raina asked, running her finger over her lips as she thought.

"Yes, but why would they do that, and why use Spencer?" Haro questioned.

"And someone who can create those kinds of illusions is rare," Kayla reasoned. "They would have to be very powerful."

There was something in the way Kayla said this that rubbed Liv the wrong way. She shook it off, strode past the other warrior, and took her spot. "I was actually coming to the council today to give a report. Father Time and I believe that our enemies aren't gone."

Again the council stirred, many of them whispering. However, Kayla continued to stare at Liv. "We will always have enemies. That goes with the territory of policing the magical world."

"Yeah," Liv said, her tone agreeable. "But whoever this is seems to still have a vendetta against mortals, very much the same as Adler Sinclair's."

Kayla sat back with a look of annoyance on her face.

"What evidence do you have?" Bianca asked, her nostrils flaring.

"Well, for starters, someone woke the SandMan," Liv explained.

Again, collective muttering. The council was like a bunch of excited schoolchildren about to go on a field trip, Liv thought.

"*The* SandMan?" Hester asked. "That's why mortals have been falling asleep randomly, isn't it? We thought it might have something to do with their brains being over-loaded by the sudden appearance of magic, but the Sand-Man! That makes much more sense."

"How do you know the SandMan was actually awakened?" Kayla asked.

"Because I put him back to sleep," Liv stated.

"And where is he?" Kayla asked, studying her tablet. "I don't see anything in your report about it."

"Yes, because it was a case for Father Time," Liv stated. "I'm not at liberty to say."

Kayla lowered her tablet, a ruthless glare in her eyes. *Oh, there was the family resemblance to Adler Sinclair,* Liv thought. *Now I see it.*

"If the SandMan has been moved, that is of interest to the council," Kayla argued.

"He's safe and asleep, and that's all anyone needs to know," Liv said definitively.

"Actually," Hester began, "I think it's best if few know the SandMan's whereabouts. It's better if you keep that information to yourself."

"Well, and not to mention that your cases with Father Time are off the record," Raina stated.

"I really must object," Kayla said. "Where are the checks and balances if we can't review your work?"

Clark laughed. It was strange for him to do that, so everyone turned in his direction. "Really, who wants to have Father Time as a boss? I don't think we have to worry about micromanaging Liv. I'm certain the little guy is doing that on his own."

Liv flashed him a punishing look. Only a few knew the current form Papa Creola had taken. It was best if not many knew since he was fearful that others were hunting him, both to make requests and for other selfish gains. Clark's laughter ended abruptly as he read the murderous expression on Liv's face.

"I am only guessing, though," Clark quickly covered. "I'm not sure if he's little or not."

Right on cue, Diabolos squawked, throwing doubt on Clark's words. Liv rubbed her hand over her forehead, trying to decide exactly when she was going to put her brother into a headlock.

Hester glared at the crow before bringing her attention back to Liv. "It's good to hear that mortals are safe once more, and you bring up a good point. If someone woke the SandMan, they definitely are going after mortals."

"Are we sure it couldn't have been something Adler did before he was stopped?" Haro asked.

"I don't know how we can be sure of anything," Liv stated. "However, I think it's important that we keep up our guard in case there are others out there who want to undermine the House of Fourteen's agenda." Her eyes flicked to Spencer, who, as before, appeared to be in a strange daze.

"And what about your task of finding the Mortal Seven?" Bianca asked. "Have you made any progress with that, or have you only been supposedly hunting down the SandMan?"

Her message was so riddled with insinuations. Liv had to stop herself from saying something that would only bring further heat onto her. However, she had to get in at least one jab. "Well, tracking down the SandMan wasn't as easy as picking out shoes to go with my funeral costume," Liv said, flicking her hand in Bianca's direction.

The Councilor narrowed her eyes, looking down at her black dress, which was buttoned all the way up to the neck. "Insulting my clothes? Have you really sunk so low?"

"I have," Liv admitted at once. "And yes, I've made progress with the Mortal Seven case. I'm hoping the first one will be found tonight."

This was a rather hopeful promise on Liv's part, but she had to believe it was John. If she sang the chimera song to Pickles and he didn't transform, well, she'd be extremely disappointed. Although she'd tried to prepare herself for this potential reality, she also thought there was great power in believing in her desired outcome.

"Tonight?" Kayla asked. "And which one of the Mortal Seven families are you going after?"

A chill ran down Liv's spine. She had the urge to erase the names of the Mortal Seven families from the record, but that would be impossible. They were clearly printed on the tree in the chamber behind the council.

"The Luce family," Liv lied.

Diabolos squawked loudly.

Liv shot him a frustrated scowl. "Did I say tonight? I meant tomorrow."

Kayla leaned back with a satisfied grin on her face. "Well, I wish you the best of luck with that."

Liv lowered her chin, wishing that she had the ability to see through illusions. "I don't need luck."

CHAPTER THIRTY-SEVEN

Liv was hoping to swing by John's shop before her big plans for later. She had an extra half-hour. Her insides were nearly bursting with excitement. She simply had to know if Pickles was a chimera.

However, when she rounded the corner, she noticed a figure pacing in front of the repair shop. Liv stopped suddenly wondering what that person was doing here. He didn't belong there, and it was obvious by the way many passersby gave him curious stares.

"What are you doing here?" Liv asked Emilio Mantovani as she approached.

Much like his sister, he was wearing all black. However, he didn't give her the same repulsed stare as Bianca. "I need your help."

Liv sighed. "Get in line, then."

She charged past him into the shop, looking around anxiously for John and Pickles. Emilio, who couldn't take a hint, strode into the shop after her. "I'm serious, Liv. I really need help, and I think you're the only one who can do it."

"I have no idea how to get it out," Liv said, spinning to face him.

His face contorted in confusion. "Get what out?"

"The stick up your sister's ass," she answered with a snicker. "I fear it is stuck up there for good."

To her surprise, he laughed at that. "My sister is really uptight. That's actually one of the reasons I need your help."

"This is about the fae girl you like, isn't it?" Liv asked.

"I love her," Emilio corrected.

"That's part of the fae's deception, you realize?"

He shook his head. "Electra wouldn't do that to me. What I feel for her is real. What we have is pure."

"That's beautiful," Liv said sarcastically. "There's a pharmacy down the street. Go down there, buy a sappy greeting card, write that on the inside, and give it to her. Girls love that sort of thing, or so I've heard."

"Liv, you know that I can't even see her," Emilio stated. "Bianca has forbidden it."

"I get that she likes to act like an authoritative school mistress, and dress like one too, but she has no power over you." Liv absentmindedly glanced around, looking for John in the back or Pickles resting in his bed. There was no sign of them.

"She does, though," Emilio said, following Liv around the shop. "She's the Councilor, and therefore can demote me if she chooses."

Liv halted suddenly. "She wouldn't."

He nodded. "She would, and has promised to replace

me if I don't stop seeing Electra. There are other eligible Mantovanis who can take my place."

Liv shook her head. The council had way too much power if they could simply uproot a Warrior without a good excuse. "Well, that sucks, but I don't know what you want me to do about it. Bianca won't do anything I say. Actually, if I argued with her about it, that would only make her more likely to pursue it."

"Please don't let this go to your head, but you have a tenacious spirit that can't be beat."

Liv rolled her eyes. "You, Mantovani, really don't know how to talk to people, do you?"

"I think you're okay and all. I don't hate you like my sister does."

"This Electra girl. Is she deaf? Or did she fall for this smooth sweet-talking you do?"

Emilio shook his head. "Liv, I'm trying to say that you're the only one I can think of who can change things. For too long, the laws of the House have stated that there could be no interracial relations between Royals and other magical creatures."

Liv sighed. "Yes, I'm aware of how outdated and conservative the laws are."

"That's exactly why we have to change them," Emilio said with enthusiasm. "The House is different now. We are the House of Fourteen. Soon the Mortal Seven will join us. We should update our laws. We need to innovate ourselves for the twenty-first century."

"Great. That's a lovely speech," Liv said. "Please give it to the council."

He sighed loudly. "I can't. Bianca would kill me. However, *you* have nothing to lose."

She lowered her chin, ready to spell the uncouth magician. "I have plenty to lose."

"Yes, but you don't seem to care," he argued. "You went up against Adler. You're not afraid to speak your mind. You're the perfect person to change things."

"I'm sort of busy right now recovering the Mortal Seven," Liv said, noticing a note on the worktable addressed to her. She plucked it up.

"I get that. I was just thinking that maybe in between doing what you do, you could also help to change the laws," Emilio said, a begging quality in his voice.

Liv was only giving him a hard time. She had every intention of helping him. And not only that, she had to change the laws for her and Stefan. The question was how. And hopefully, Clark and Raina would have some answers about that.

After leaving Emilio in uncomfortable silence for a long bit, she brought her eyes away from the note John left for her. "Fine. I'll help you."

His fist shot in the air. "Thank you. I knew you would. You really aren't an undisciplined obnoxious heathen."

"Thanks," Liv said dryly, pointing to the door and dismissing Emilio. He left without a word, giving Liv a chance to read the note John had left for her since he apparently didn't believe in text messages.

I'm at the apartment. Join me when you return.

Liv huffed in frustration. Singing to Pickles would have to wait.

CHAPTER THIRTY-EIGHT

"I think I'm losing all my brain cells," Rudolf said, pausing after trying to blow up a balloon.

"Now you know how the rest of us feel," Liv said dryly, holding up a long bit of streamer as Rory hung it on the wall.

"Why, again, can't we use magic to decorate for Sophia's party?" Rudolf asked.

"Because," Bermuda stated, grabbing the balloon he'd failed multiple times to blow up. "It's more special if we actually put physical effort into decorating. It means more."

"Also, apparently Leonard doesn't do well with too much magic performed around him," Liv said, indicating the first bathroom.

"Leonard?" Rudolf questioned, sticking his finger into the cheese dip and tasting it.

"That's Liv's way of trying to nickname Sophia's dragon," Stefan stated.

"It's cute, and he totally loves it," Liv said, slapping Rudolf's hand away as he tried to sample the dip again.

"I'm certain he doesn't," Bermuda countered. "Dragons are refined, and usually don't like humor."

"But those are dragons raised by other dragons," Rory countered, taping the streamer in place. He gave Liv an impatient look since she'd abandoned her post, helping him.

"I don't see why it would be any different for Sophia's dragon," Bermuda stated in a nasal voice.

"Because sometimes when we aren't raised around our kind, we behave a bit differently," Rory said in a low voice.

"Are you insinuating something, son?" Bermuda questioned, her voice rising.

"When did you say, John, that Sophia had left to take Pickles on his walk?" Liv asked loudly, trying to interrupt the feud about to ensue.

John pulled his head out the mess of wires around the entertainment center. He'd been trying to get the music going, but there were some technical difficulties. "I think—"

"I don't see why dogs can't walk themselves," Serena said, practicing the Charleston in the middle of the floor.

"And I'm astonished that you don't need to be walked," Liv said.

"Now, are you sure that if I keep this up, it will enhance my fertility?" Serena asked Bermuda.

The giant nodded. Then she leaned over and whispered to Liv, "No, actually. I just needed to get that annoying girl out of my hair. She doesn't stop."

"She makes me look pretty okay, right?" Liv questioned.

Bermuda thought about that for a moment, then shook

her head. "Oh, no. But speaking of hair, have you been washing yours with dish soap? It looks really dry."

"Swamp water," Liv corrected, still looking in John's direction.

Noticing her concern, he said, "She should be back any moment now."

"Okay, I want everyone in their places," Liv stated. "Sophia will be back soon, and I want this to be a genuine surprise."

John pushed up from the floor with great effort, his breathing heavy. "I think that might work. Try it again, Liv."

She threw her finger in the direction of the stereo, and music filled the air. Liv had compiled a playlist with all of Sophia's favorite songs. She'd also made sure the party was stocked with all her favorite foods. However, something appeared to be missing.

"Clark?" Liv called toward the kitchen.

"I'm coming," her brother said, backing into the living area, holding a three-tiered cake. It was as beautiful as one of Sophia's dresses, covered in pastels and dripping with vines and flowers.

"Wow, where did you get it?" Stefan asked.

Clark shot him a look of offense. "I didn't buy it. I made it. I've been dabbling with cake-making."

"Of course, you have," Liv said, shaking her head at him. "It's beautiful."

"Thank you," he said, carefully sliding the cake onto the buffet of food. As he stood back, he whispered over his shoulder to Liv, "And don't worry. I'm not too busy with this new hobby to look into that thing you wanted me to."

She nodded discreetly. Stefan, on the other side of her, gave her a hopeful look.

"You mean that law you need to change so Liv and Stefan can snog?" Rudolf asked loudly.

"Oh, I think Serena ate the potpourri again," Liv said loudly. "She looks a bit green."

The mortal grabbed her stomach, indeed appearing sick. "I don't feel so well."

"Okay, well, go down the hall to the second bathroom," Liv instructed.

Serena turned, fleeing as the door swung open and Sophia and Pickles bounded through.

"Surprise!" the gang yelled, but no one got out the word all the way before they lost their voices from the sight of the girl who was supposed to be nine years old.

In the space of half an hour, she appeared to have aged a full year. She gave everyone a wide smile, curtseying. "Surprise!"

CHAPTER THIRTY-NINE

"Sophia, what happened?" Liv exclaimed, rushing forward and grabbing her sister by the shoulders as Pickles ran for his master.

The young magician looked down at her dress, which had fit earlier but was now tight around the waist and a bit short. "I'm not sure."

Liv glanced up, finding Rory in the crowd. He read the expression in her eyes and seemed to know at once what she was thinking. With a quick pivot, he strode for the first bathroom, which was where they were currently keeping the dragon egg. When he returned a moment later, his eyes were wide with excitement. "It's gotten bigger."

"Gotten bigger?" Liv questioned. "Like, it still fits in the bathtub?"

"Barely," he answered.

Liv turned her attention back to Sophia. "How do you feel?"

Sophia blushed, noticing all the faces staring at her. "I'm fine. I'm really grateful for the birthday party."

"It looks like we owe you two," Liv stated. "How long were you gone?"

"It's the dragon egg," Bermuda said, striding forward and placing a hand on Sophia's head. After a moment, she nodded like she'd done a full diagnostic on the girl. "Yes. As I suspected, her dragon is trying to get her ready for his hatching."

"So he's speeding up her growth?" Clark exclaimed, shaking his head.

"Well, you can't expect him to hatch for a young magician," Bermuda stated. "No, he'll want someone at the same level of maturity as him."

"But he's currently in an egg, so I think Sophia is a bit ahead of him," Liv argued.

"Yes, but as we already know," Bermuda began, "he can talk and hear and sense things. He's very advanced. And once he hatches, he'll have more experience than most young adults."

"But our Sophia…" Liv said, pressing the girl into her.

She gripped her back. "Liv, I know. But I'm totally fine. What just happened to me felt like the most natural thing in the world, although it did leave me really hungry."

"The dip is good," Rudolf said with his mouth full.

"Shouldn't you be checking on your bride?" Stefan suggested.

"Oh! Right!" Rudolf sped toward the second bathroom.

"Well, welcome to your party," Liv said, holding her arms out wide.

Sophia beamed. "You all are the best. Thank you so much! I had no idea." She hurried off to fill her plate with food.

Liv retreated a few steps, needing a moment to process this. She had just gotten Sophia back, and now she was literally growing up before her eyes. Internally, she was conflicted on so many levels about this dragon-riding business. It was what Sophia wanted, so there would be no further questions asked, but if Liv did have a say…well, she wouldn't say a thing.

When you loved someone, you supported them, even if their endeavors filled your heart with a fear that kept you up at night.

CHAPTER FORTY

Liv waited until she'd tucked Sophia into her bed to sneak out of the apartment. Even if her little sister had grown up a full year inside half an hour, she was still a child, and fell asleep without protest after a night of dancing, laughing, and eating Clark's scrumptious cake.

Confident that Clark or Rudolf or Rory or any of the others sleeping in her now-large place would wake up if Sophia needed something, Liv set off for John's apartment, which was next to hers. He opened the door a bit bleary-eyed, having left the party over an hour before, stating he "was an old mortal who couldn't keep up with the magical folks."

"Is everything okay?" he asked, peeling the door back at the sight of her.

"Yes, it's fine," she said, peering down to find Pickles licking her feet. "Can I please come in?"

"Well, of course." John stood back, waving her into his modest apartment. It used to be double the size of hers, but he'd refused to have renovations made on it, and therefore

229

it was still the same as the first time she'd seen it five years prior when he'd offered her a job and a place to stay.

"I have to think that something is wrong if you're here at this late hour," John said, shutting the door behind her.

"Nothing is wrong, John. It's just that I can't wait another minute to find out the truth."

"The truth?" John asked, following her into the apartment. "About what?"

"I need to know if you're one of the Mortal Seven," she explained.

He scratched his receding hairline and shrugged. "Well, I don't know. I'm fairly certain I'm just a boring old mortal."

Liv shook her head. "No, you're better than any mortal I've ever met. Hell, you're better than most magicians I've ever met. And you far exceed fae and filthy elves, although I love all people. Anyway, my point is that you're fair beyond reason. You want a better world, which is why you repair things instead of allowing them to go into the landfill. And you tolerate me even when I'm a pain in the butt—"

"You're never a pain," he interrupted.

She offered him a grateful smile. "John, I'm not sure if this is right, but you seem to make my magic stronger. When I first came into my powers after becoming a Warrior, you seemed to help me balance them. If my instinct is right on this, you're no normal mortal. You do for me what I think the Mortal Seven are supposed to do for the House of Fourteen."

He chuckled. "I appreciate the compliment, but what if you're wrong?"

"I've considered that a lot lately," Liv said. "It's possible I've blown this up in my mind. However, my father said that if something looks like a skunk and smells like a skunk, then it probably is one."

"So, is this your way of telling me to shower?"

Liv laughed. "No, it's my way of saying I think you're different. Well, we know you are. You're definitely in one of the Mortal Seven families, but I believe you are *one* of the Mortal Seven."

"Okay, but why now? Why are you so concerned about figuring this out now?"

"Because I think I know how," Liv said. She pointed at the Jack Russell terrier at her feet, who had his tongue hanging out of his mouth and that same hyper expression he usually regarded her with. "You've had Pickles since I met you, right?"

John seemed thrown off by this question. "Well, yeah. Pickles was why we talked. I remember the day I met you outside the shop. You were dressed in that black hoodie and staring around like you were lost. I was just going to dismiss you as some hoodlum, casing the shop."

"Hey, now!" Liv protested.

John waved her off. "But Pickles ran straight up to you and jumped up on your leg. He only does that with people who are good through and through, so I knew you were all right. Then we got to talking, and you said you were looking for work and a place to live, and as they say, the rest is history."

Liv nodded, remembering the moment clearly. "And how long have you had Pickles?"

The dog tilted his head to the side like he was considering this question too.

John tapped his finger on his chin. "Oh, it's been a long time. I got him right before I opened the shop. I'm trying to remember when that was."

"John, you've had the shop for over thirty years!"

He gave her an astonished expression. "Yeah, you're right. Pickles showed up on my doorstep soon after Chloe left me."

John frowned as the thought of his magician ex-wife drifted across his mind.

"John, you're telling me this dog is over thirty years old, and you've never thought twice about it?" Liv asked in disbelief.

He bent down and patted the terrier on the head. "Well, I feed him only the best, and we have three walks a day, although my knees are starting to bother me of late, so maybe we'll scale them back to two."

Liv shook her head. "It doesn't matter what you feed a dog. For him to be over thirty years old is unheard of."

"Well, what are you saying?" John asked, confusion making the wrinkles on his face deepen.

"John, each of the Mortal Seven is guarded by a magical animal," Liv began. "I've spent some time tracking down the way to make these seemingly normal animals take their actual form. I firmly believe Pickles is your chimera."

"Which means?" John asked.

"If he is, it's a hundred percent certainty that you're one of the Mortal Seven."

John combed his hand over his head, suddenly looking serious. "My Pickles. You think he's this Camaro?"

"Chimera," Liv corrected. "And maybe. Or you're just the best dog owner in the world. But there's only one way to find out."

John looked at the dog and then Liv several times. "Okay. I guess I'll never be really ready for this moment. Do what you've got to do."

Liv took a step back, not sure exactly the words of the song Rooster gave to her.

"Wait," John interrupted as she tried to find the tune in her head.

"What?" Liv asked.

"If Pickles changes, will he always be…well, you know, *different*? I'm not sure I can explain that to my customers."

"Well, remember that magic is real for everyone now," Liv said with a smile. "But one of the things I learned from Bermuda is that chimeras have the ability to shift to their regular form and a more acceptable one. It's just that the ones attached to the Mortal Seven have been locked in their disguises because magic was hidden from mortals. I think it was to preserve them and protect the Seven."

John nodded. "Okay, well, do your hocus pocus then. I hope it doesn't hurt."

Liv smiled. "I don't think you'll feel a thing."

She knelt and petted Pickles on the head. The sweet dog licked her fingers, and strangely, the words she couldn't remember flowed effortlessly off her tongue. She heard herself singing, and even without music accompanying her voice, she sounded beautiful. The words she sang were hard to understand, and yet their message was something she knew in her heart: All is love.

When the words ran out, Liv pushed back to her feet.

"Liv, I had no idea you could sing," John said, smiling at her.

"I couldn't until recently."

"Is that it?" John asked.

Liv studied the dog, who was staring up at her expectantly. "I don't know. I haven't done this before."

"Well, nothing has seemed to happen. What does that mean?"

Liv sighed. "I think it means you're not one of the Mortal Seven, but it doesn't change anything. You're still the best mortal in the world."

John's eyes twinkled. "Well, I appreciate that. And I'm sure you'll find your Carraway for the House of Fourteen. It just isn't me."

Liv nodded, her heart heavy. "I'll let you get some sleep. I'm sorry for bothering you so late."

He waved her off. "Don't be. Actually, I'm feeling quite awake now." He slapped his knees, looking down at Pickles. "Who would like a bonus walk?"

The dog yelped.

"It's settled," John stated, grabbing the leash from the countertop. "We will walk you out. A bit of fresh air will do me good."

Liv nodded, not saying another word as she watched Pickles twirl, excited to go on a late-night walk.

"Well, hold still, would you?" John urged.

The dog barked at him, making him laugh even more.

"Are you sure about the extra walk?" Liv asked. "What about your knee?"

He tested it. "It actually feels really good right now."

"I'm glad for that," Liv said. "Maybe it was Clark's cake."

"Yes, and all your friend's positive energy," John said, picking up the keys for the door as they exited.

When they were in the hallway of the apartment, Liv forced a smile on her face. "Well, thanks for humoring me, John. You and Pickles have a good night. I'll see you in the morning."

"Why don't you sleep in?" he suggested.

"But I always open," she argued.

"Yeah, but I think you need to sleep. And I'd like to get down there early and work on some projects." There was new excitement buzzing behind John's eyes.

"Okay, well, whatever you want. I'm sure Sophia would like the chance to cuddle up and watch cartoons."

"Yes," John stated with a smile. "You spend the time with that lovely girl. I'll see you when you get in."

"Thanks, John," Liv said, turning for her apartment. She was almost to her door when John exclaimed, making her spin back around.

"What is it?" Liv didn't have to wait for his answer to know what had startled him.

He was standing right where she'd left him, holding onto Pickles' leash, but John suddenly appeared to be ten years younger.

Liv rushed over. "John, what happened?"

He felt his face. Ran his hands over his head, which was no longer mostly bald. Shook his head. "I don't know. I suddenly felt taller and more energetic. How do I look?"

She nodded. "You're younger."

When he smiled, the usual wrinkles didn't spring to his eyes. "Well, I'll be. How did you do that?"

Liv shook her head. "I don't know. Sophia is getting

older, and meanwhile, you're getting younger. It doesn't make any—"

She didn't get a chance to finish her sentence because right then, Pickles transformed, growing to three times his size. His face morphed until it was that of a lion. His tail elongated, a serpent's head forming on its end. Pickle's entire body contorted, taking on several appearances until it was rippling with muscles. And from his back sprouted the neck and head of a goat.

Liv had never seen a creature so strange and yet so beautiful. And what set it off, nearly making her burst out laughing, was that John was still holding onto the leash like he was going to take the little dog for a walk.

"Well, this is odd," John said, looking at his pet and Liv in quiet disbelief.

She squealed, racing forward and throwing her arms around John. His frame wasn't boney like it had been before. He was strong, and hugged her back. Realizing that the magic trapped in his chimera had somehow healed him, Liv released John and then threw her arms around Pickles. "Thank you, thank you, thank you!" she rejoiced.

The chimera purred against her, as gentle as when he had been a terrier, pressing his soft mane into her face.

When she released the magical creature, she was surprised to find tears streaming down her cheeks.

"Oh, now, what are you crying about?" John asked, seeming more surprised by her tears than by the fact that his thirty-year-old terrier had been a magical creature in disguise. "Is it because this proves that I'm a Mortal Seven?"

Liv nodded and then shook her head. "It proves that,

meaning my normal life has just collided with my magical one. But that's not all."

He smiled sympathetically at her. "Liv, I think we both know you've never had two separate lives. You only ever thought you did."

She was astonished at how strangely wise he sounded. It was John's voice, but he was different somehow; well, besides looking ten years younger. "But John, the chimera is supposed to protect its Mortal Seven. That's why you're younger."

"I'm younger? Are you sure?" he asked, running his hand over his head again. "I thought I felt more hair up there. Are you positive?"

She conjured a mirror and handed it to him, holding her breath as he peered into it.

His eyes widened in shock. "Well, I'll be. I look better than when I've slept for twelve hours!"

"And that means releasing the chimera has healed you. John, you'll live longer now, and you'll help us to protect magic, as I realize now was always a part of your destiny."

John seemed momentarily knocked off-guard by this. Then he looked at Pickles, who was almost eye to eye with him. The mortal didn't appear shocked to be looking into the eyes of a lion he had previously thought was only his little terrier. Instead, he reached out and tousled the top of his head, the way he always did to Pickles. "When we have good friends, they make us feel healthier, younger, and like we can take on the world."

CHAPTER FORTY-ONE

Talon was tired of living in the Black Void. He was ready to leave it, but the time wasn't right. Father Time needed to be found. Killed. And Kayla had much work to do.

"Master," she said, striding through the dark space now lined with orbs of light. Her white hair glowed around her heart-shaped face.

"Olivia Beaufont put the SandMan back to sleep," he nearly yelled, his fury rocking the ground under their feet.

"I know," she said in a rush, kneeling before the God Magician. "When she killed my illusion of Spencer, it momentarily knocked me out. By the time I recovered, she had already gotten away with Zeno Dutillet."

Talon swept back and forth, his robe brushing the bones of rodents and larger animals. "If she awakes the Mortal Seven and brings them all into the House of Seven, everything I've worked for will be gone!"

Kayla visibly shook. "I know, Grandfather. I'm willing to do whatever you ask to stop her."

"Gone!" he repeated. "Already, I feel part of me dying, which means she's found one of the Mortal Seven."

"But master, you seem so much stronger," Kayla argued.

"Strength has nothing to do with life force," he explained. "I stole my life from the ones I took, but when they come back, it will end my long reign. I can't live while the Mortal Seven do."

"I'll stop her," Kayla said eagerly. "Just tell me what you'd have me do? Spencer is a pawn. Only an illusion. I can send him to do my bidding. The girl they know as Kayla isn't real either. I can fool them. I know I can."

He nodded slowly. Adler had been a failure. Decar had only been an average magician. But Kayla? She was a grandchild he could be proud of. "You must track down the Mortal Seven families and destroy them before Olivia Beaufont does. Every second counts."

"I'll do it, my lord. I promise."

The smile that spread across Talon's face lacked joy. It was full of greed and fury. It was the thing that fueled wars. "Good, because, Kayla, you're are my last hope. If you fail, I'll have to resort to the most drastic measures."

Book 9! Wow! I've never written nine books in a series before. It is all thanks to you, the reader. Yes, you. The one reading these words right now. This word. And this one. Okay, I'm sorry. I'll stop. But seriously, you're the one who has read the 8 books before this. Has supported, reviewed, and cheered me on to keep writing the series. Without you, this wouldn't be happening. Believe me. I've had series that didn't go past a certain point because it just didn't have the same steam as the Unstoppable Liv Beaufont. You like the series and for that, I'm exceptionally grateful. Thank you!

I'm excited for this next arc. I'm going to dare to say I think it will be better than the first two. For one, this chimera thing has me silly excited. Michael and I came up with that idea over video com and I was so eager that I nearly dropped off the call so I could get started on writing. There's a story that came out of that call that will come a little later (next Author's Notes). Michael will regret ever telling me anything about his childhood. I get it though. I was a kid once and made mistakes. Nothing like this though. Anyway, when my friend, Michael, confided in me this story about something he did, I did what most would do and took notes and planned to put it into book 10. Later, I'll further add insult to injury by highlighting it in the author notes. Stay tuned.

As many of you know, Lydia, my daughter, helps me to craft storylines (usually over breakfast). In the original outline, Rooster wasn't in the book. But then book 9 would have been way shorter. Anyway, we crafted the Rooster storyline one morning. Remember the chickens that her father got her that I had to watch? That's where the inspiration for Alicia the chicken came from. Well, one of those chicks turned out to be a rooster, which got my ex in trouble with his neighborhood. Anyway, when I was looking for names for this character, Lydia threw out Rooster and I thought it was perfect for a musician.

I used to live in Southern Oregon and have some really amazing readers there who I like to throw in Easter eggs for every now and then. One year, I hiked up to the top of Mount McLaughlin, one of the highest peaks in the Rogue Valley area. Places I've been are always great locations for stories. That's one reason I decided to use that as the location for Rooster's castle.

And then Lydia wanted him to be a musician. I've talked about the beauty of inspiration before and how it surprises me all the time. This storyline was another instance of that. I got into writing those chapters and was blown away with how perfect a broken-hearted musician worked for this. And then the ending.

Those familiar with the Rogue Valley know that one of the largest employers for a long time was a company called

Musician's Friend. My ex actually used to work there and I have a ton of friends that were connected with the company. A few dozen of us actually moved to the LA area together and have a bond because of that. Anyway, I was blown away when finishing up the Rooster chapter when he turned to Liv and said, "You're a musician's friend." It gave me chills because I never even planned that but it couldn't have been more perfect.

Rooster's band name is Moldy Oranges. When Lydia and I were coming with up ideas and I said, "Well, what's the band name going to be?" She answered, "Of course it has to be Moldy Oranges." I was like, "Of course!"

We have an orange tree in the backyard. I'm too short to properly get the oranges before they go bad most of the time. Or the squirrels take a bite and throw them on the patio (because they want me to kill them. (MA can I borrow your bb gun?)).

Anyway, often I can be found cleaning up moldy oranges in the backyard. And on many occasions, as I'm doing that and cursing at squirrels, I've said, "If I ever have a band, I'm calling it Moldy Oranges." And that's where ideas come from.

Okay, I'm off to start book 10 and looking forward to inspiration lending me breath-taking moments. Thank you again for being awesome.

THANK YOU for not only reading this story but these *Author Notes* **as well.**

(I think I've been good with always opening with "thank you." If not, I need to edit the other *Author Notes*!)

RANDOM (*sometimes*) THOUGHTS?

Orange Trees and Moldy Oranges.

Ok, for most of my life I have never had a fruit tree. I didn't particularly mind not having a fruit tree because the only fruit I like is Lime Jello.

(Wait, can I include Kool-Aid? Because I'll drink the hell out of a lot of fruit-flavored Kool-Aid's. Now, I'm almost embarrassed to admit at 51 years old I love Kool-Aid, but since I'm 51 years old I also don't really care what people think, either.)

Ok, back to fruit trees.

Now I have a house that has three fruit trees (orange, fig, and lemon.) We have moldy oranges, and I hate them.

Why can't fruit trees grow fruit, and if no one eats them, they disappear?

Ok, I realize the animals and need to propagate can't allow this to be, but moldy oranges suck.

Never Share Your Secrets.

I know the story Sarah is talking about that she is going to share. I'm forever embarrassed about this story and so know it comes out I'll hate it (cause I was an ass.)

(Well, it won't come out not now-now although I could just share it and mess with her - I won't because it's obvious she needs this Machiavellian emotional outlet - so I'll wait for it to show up later.)

Sometimes (as a kid) you shouldn't give in to your desire to prove your skills.

AROUND THE WORLD IN 80 DAYS

One of the interesting (at least to me) aspects of my life is the ability to work from anywhere and at any time. In the future, I hope to re-read my own *Author Notes* and remember my life as a diary entry.

605 Freeway heading to Los Angeles International Airport (LAX)

Tippity-typing my way along in stop and go traffic listening to the driver speak with my wife about scammers causing crashes with professional drivers.

Usually, I'm interested in listening to this type of information because it is a window into another person's life. At the moment, I'm too sleepy to care.

I'm about to close my eyes… I want to so bad.

Maybe I'll dream of a way to get Sarah back and I'll snicker in my sleep.

I doubt it. My dreams are too nice.

Remind me (next time) that collaborating with Sarah is a two-edged sword.

FAN PRICING

$0.99 Saturdays (new LMBPN stuff) and $0.99 Wednesday (both LMBPN books and friends of LMBPN books.) Get great stuff from us and others at tantalizing prices.

Go ahead, I bet you can't read just one.

Sign up here: http://lmbpn.com/email/.

HOW TO MARKET FOR BOOKS YOU LOVE

Review them so others have your thoughts, tell friends and the dogs of your enemies (because who wants to talk with enemies?)… *Enough said ;-)*

Ad Aeternitatem,

Michael Anderle

ACKNOWLEDGMENTS

SARAH NOFFKE

My favorite part of writing any book is creating the acknowledgements page. It reminds me that writing a book is not a solo task. I might sit alone and write, but the finished product is a result of the support and encouragement of a tribe of people.

Thank you to the readers who buy the books, read them, review and recommend. YOU are the one who keeps us writing. I'm always inspired by the messages I receive from readers. Thank you supporting the books and offering so much richness to my life.

Thank you to my LBMPN family for all the support. Steve, Michael, Lynne, Moonchild, Jennifer and so many others who help champion the book to publication and beyond.

Thank you to the beta readers who offered so many valuable insights early on. Thank you to John, Chrisa, Kelly, Martin and Larry.

Thank you to the JIT team for all the awesome feedback. A new series is always exciting and nerve-wracking.

Michael and I thought we had a great idea for a new world, but we don't really know until we get objective feedback. What would I do without all you awesome readers?

Thank you to my friends and family. Writing is a strange profession. I work weird hours, talk to myself, have a strange diet, get antsy about deadlines. But the wonderful people in my life continue to show their encouragement and thoughtfulness no matter what. It is never lost on me because I know that I wouldn't be doing what I love without all you amazing people, cheering me on.

And as with all my books, the final thank you goes to my muse, Lydia. I wrote my first book so that I could make my daughter proud, and it's never stopped. I write every book for you, my love.

Sarah Noffke writes YA and NA science fiction, fantasy, paranormal and urban fantasy. In addition to being an author, she is a mother, podcaster and professor. Noffke holds a Masters of Management and teaches college business/writing courses. Most of her students have no idea that she toils away her hours crafting fictional characters. www.sarahnoffke.com

Check out other work by Sarah author <u>here</u>.

Ghost Squadron:

<u>Formation #1:</u>

Kill the bad guys. Save the Galaxy. All in a hard day's work.

After ten years of wandering the outer rim of the galaxy, Eddie Teach is a man without a purpose. He was one of the toughest pilots in the Federation, but now he's just a regular guy, getting into bar fights and making a difference wherever he can. It's not the same as flying a ship and saving colonies, but it'll have to do.

That is, until General Lance Reynolds tracks Eddie down and offers him a job. There are bad people out there, plotting terrible things, killing innocent people, and destroying entire colonies. **Someone has to stop them.**

Eddie, along with the genetically-enhanced combat pilot Julianna Fregin and her trusty E.I. named Pip, must recruit a diverse team of specialists, both human and alien. They'll need to master their new Q-Ship, one of the most powerful strike ships ever constructed. And finally, they'll have to stop a faceless enemy so powerful, it threatens to destroy the entire Federation.

All in a day's work, right?

Experience this exciting military sci-fi saga and the latest addition to the expanded Kurtherian Gambit Universe. If you're a fan of Mass Effect, Firefly, or Star Wars, you'll love this riveting new space opera.

NOTE: If cursing is a problem, then this might not be for you.

Check out the entire series <u>here</u>.

The Precious Galaxy Series:

Corruption #1

A new evil lurks in the darkness.

After an explosion, the crew of a battlecruiser mysteriously disappears.

Bailey and Lewis, complete strangers, find themselves

suddenly onboard the damaged ship. Lewis hasn't worked a case in years, not since the final one broke his spirit and his bank account. The last thing Bailey remembers is preparing to take down a fugitive on Onyx Station.

Mysteries are harder to solve when there's no evidence left behind.

Bailey and Lewis don't know how they got onboard *Ricky Bobby* or why. However, they quickly learn that whatever was responsible for the explosion and disappearance of the crew is still on the ship.

Monsters are real and what this one can do changes everything.

The new team bands together to discover what happened and how to fight the monster lurking in the bottom of the battlecruiser.

Will they find the missing crew? Or will the monster end them all?

The Soul Stone Mage Series:

House of Enchanted #1:

The Kingdom of Virgo has lived in peace for thousands of years...until now.

The humans from Terran have always been real assholes to the witches of Virgo. Now a silent war is brewing, and the timing couldn't be worse. Princess Azure will soon be crowned queen of the Kingdom of Virgo.

In the Dark Forest a powerful potion-maker has been murdered.

Charmsgood was the only wizard who could stop a

deadly virus plaguing Virgo. He also knew about the devastation the people from Terran had done to the forest.

Azure must protect her people. Mend the Dark Forest. Create alliances with savage beasts. No biggie, right?

But on coronation day everything changes. Princess Azure isn't who she thought she was and that's a big freaking problem.

Welcome to The Revelations of Oriceran. Check out the entire series here.

The Lucidites Series:

Awoken, #1:
Around the world humans are hallucinating after sleepless nights.

In a sterile, underground institute the forecasters keep reporting the same events.

And in the backwoods of Texas, a sixteen-year-old girl is about to be caught up in a fierce, ethereal battle.

Meet Roya Stark. She drowns every night in her dreams, spends her hours reading classic literature to avoid her family's ridicule, and is prone to premonitions—which are becoming more frequent. And now her dreams are filled with strangers offering to reveal what she has always wanted to know: Who is she? That's the question that haunts her, and she's about to find out. But will Roya live to regret learning the truth?

Stunned, #2
Revived, #3

The Reverians Series:

Defects, #1:

In the happy, clean community of Austin Valley, everything appears to be perfect. Seventeen-year-old Em Fuller, however, fears something is askew. Em is one of the new generation of Dream Travelers. For some reason, the gods have not seen fit to gift all of them with their expected special abilities. Em is a Defect—one of the unfortunate Dream Travelers not gifted with a psychic power. Desperate to do whatever it takes to earn her gift, she endures painful daily injections along with commands from her overbearing, loveless father. One of the few bright spots in her life is the return of a friend she had thought dead—but with his return comes the knowledge of a shocking, unforgivable truth. The society Em thought was protecting her has actually been betraying her, but she has no idea how to break away from its authority without hurting everyone she loves.

Rebels, #2

Warriors, #3

Vagabond Circus Series:

Suspended, #1:

When a stranger joins the cast of Vagabond Circus—a circus that is run by Dream Travelers and features real magic—mysterious events start happening. The once orderly grounds of the circus become riddled with hidden threats. And the ringmaster realizes not only are his circus and its magic at risk, but also his very life.

Vagabond Circus caters to the skeptics. Without skeptics, it would close its doors. This is because Vagabond

Circus runs for two reasons and only two reasons: first and foremost to provide the lost and lonely Dream Travelers a place to be illustrious. And secondly, to show the nonbelievers that there's still magic in the world. If they believe, then they care, and if they care, then they don't destroy. They stop the small abuse that day-by-day breaks down humanity's spirit. If Vagabond Circus makes one skeptic believe in magic, then they halt the cycle, just a little bit. They allow a little more love into this world. That's Dr. Dave Raydon's mission. And that's why this ringmaster recruits. That's why he directs. That's why he puts on a show that makes people question their beliefs. He wants the world to believe in magic once again.

Paralyzed, #2
Released, #3

Ren Series:

Ren: The Man Behind the Monster, #1:
Born with the power to control minds, hypnotize others, and read thoughts, Ren Lewis, is certain of one thing: God made a mistake. No one should be born with so much power. A monster awoke in him the same year he received his gifts. At ten years old. A prepubescent boy with the ability to control others might merely abuse his powers, but Ren allowed it to corrupt him. And since he can have and do anything he wants, Ren should be happy. However, his journey teaches him that harboring so much power doesn't bring happiness, it steals it. Once this realization sets in, Ren makes up his mind to do the one thing

that can bring his tortured soul some peace. He must kill the monster.

Note This book is NA and has strong language, violence and sexual references.

Ren: God's Little Monster, #2
Ren: The Monster Inside the Monster, #3
Ren: The Monster's Adventure, #3.5
Ren: The Monster's Death

Olento Research Series:

Alpha Wolf, #1:
Twelve men went missing.

Six months later they awake from drug-induced stupors to find themselves locked in a lab.

And on the night of a new moon, eleven of those men, possessed by new—and inhuman—powers, break out of their prison and race through the streets of Los Angeles until they disappear one by one into the night.

Olento Research wants its experiments back. Its CEO, Mika Lenna, will tear every city apart until he has his werewolves imprisoned once again. He didn't undertake a huge risk just to lose his would-be assassins.

However, the Lucidite Institute's main mission is to save the world from injustices. Now, it's Adelaide's job to find these mutated men and protect them and society, and fast. Already around the nation, wolflike men are being spotted. Attacks on innocent women are happening. And then, Adelaide realizes what her next step must be: She has to find the alpha wolf first. Only once she's located him can she stop whoever is behind this experiment to create wild beasts out of human beings.

<u>Lone Wolf, #2</u>
<u>Rabid Wolf, #3</u>
<u>Bad Wolf, #4</u>